MAY THE DEVIL WALK BEHIND YE!

MAY THE DEVIL WALK BEHIND YE!

Scottish Traveller Tales

Duncan Williamson

CANONGATE

First published in 1989
by Canongate Publishing Limited
17 Jeffrey Street, Edinburgh

© Duncan Williamson 1989
© Illustrations Janet Pontin 1989

The publishers acknowledge subsidy of the Scottish Arts Council
towards the publication of this volume.

British Library Cataloguing in Publication Data

Williamson, Duncan, 1928
May the devil walk behind ye;
Scottish traveller tales
I. Title
823'.914 [F]

ISBN 0–86241–214–5
ISBN 0–86241–245–5 Pbk

Typeset by Buccleuch Printers Ltd, Hawick
Printed and bound in Great Britain by
Billing & Sons Ltd, Worcester

CONTENTS

To Ailie

PREFACE

The twelve stories making up this collection from Duncan
Williamson's repertoire of folk takes are interesting because
they incorporate the Scottish travelling people's beliefs about
evil, temptation and suffering. Religious expression shines
through these stories; they are expressive of a traditional
attitude towards death. For Duncan, as for all travellers, life
is a simple force, a force deeply felt. It is spurred in the
emotive stories travellers tell and listen to about the Devil –
who opposes life and goodness.

Because of the particular function and meaning of these
stories for the Travelling People of Scotland, I have
considered it most important to write them down in the living
language of the storyteller. How to convey on paper the
vigorous form of traditional storytelling is the central
problem! Like an artist painting an old tree, I have had to
work carefully with the elements of style, line, colour, shape
and rhythm. We wish to reach a wide readership, so I have
not aimed for exact representation. I have striven most of all
for a form on paper which would show the beauty and truth
of the story, how it is nourished. Like the earth and sun to
the old tree, the traditional storyteller's words and phrases
sustain the folk tale.

As with previous publications of Duncan Williamson's
traveller tales, then, *May the Devil Walk Behind Ye!* is

closely allied to verbatim transcriptions of his storytelling. Eight of the stories were told in early 1988 to non-traveller audiences, when Duncan used Scottish English, a variety of world English. This speech is relatively easy to render in writing. But English readers may find some of the Scottish idioms, syntax and grammar unfamiliar, so the most difficult usages have been translated in footnotes. Four stories, 'Jack and the Sea Witch', 'The Miller and the Devil', 'The Devil's Coat' and 'Jack and the Devil's Gold' were recorded in 1976, 1978 and 1982 when Duncan was speaking more broad Scots, while he was still travelling and living the life of a nomad. These stories I have written down retaining their colloquialisms. Recurring Scots words, cant and dialectal terms are explained in the Glossary.

The sources of the twelve Devil stories were traditional, heard and learned by Duncan from members of his own extended family of travelling people, or from close traveller friends. His father's cousin Willie Williamson of Carradale told Duncan 'The Queen and the Devil', 'The Woodcutter and the Devil', 'Jack and the Devil's Gold', 'The Challenge', 'The Minister and the Devil' and 'Jack and the Devil's Purse'. Duncan heard these stories from old 'Uncle Willie' in Argyll when he was a boy. The Williamson family then lived in a large handmade tent or 'barrikit' in a forest near Loch Fyne. A river separated their part of the wood from another part, where travellers like Uncle Willie would come along to camp in the summer and put up their bow tents. 'We children would cross the river and go to the traveller camping places, sit there and listen,' said Duncan.

'The Devil's Coat' and 'The Devil's Salt Mill' were two stories Duncan heard from an uncle on his mother's side, Sandy Reid, who came to camp in the wood beside the Williamson family in the 1930s. 'The Henwife and the Devil' was told to Duncan and his brothers and sisters by another traveller man called John Stewart. John, who was thin with a wee crook in his neck and nicknamed the old Snowdrop, is remembered fondly by Duncan for his love of telling stories to children.

'The Tramp and the Farmer' was a favourite of Duncan's paternal grandmother, old Bet MacColl. But the story is really part of a much longer, complex narrative which features a song sung by the wife of one of the characters to her daughter, who then falls asleep and dreams the story – this story is usually all that is now told by the travellers of Argyllshire.

'Jack and the Sea Witch' and 'The Miller and the Devil' were two fine stories Duncan heard later in life after he'd left home and had a family of his own. These stories were among hundreds told by the famous traveller storyteller of Aberdeenshire: the 'Story Mannie', old Johnnie MacDonald or 'Old Toots'. He was a cripple and specialised in storytelling while watching young children for his traveller relatives, who would give him accommodation in return for his help.

Duncan Williamson knows and tells at least forty Devil stories, and there are at least twice that number which he has recalled and summarised for folklorists and traveller audiences. The final selection of stories for *May the Devil Walk Behind Ye!* includes the most popular ones told by Duncan, and ones we think will give readers the most complete and accurate picture of the Devil – what he means to the Travelling People of Scotland. 'The Challenge' and 'Jack and the Sea Witch' are not specifically about the Devil, but their ethos is quite sinister. Evil manifests itself in a variety of forms in the world! 'The Minister and the Devil' is thoroughly wicked. Its totally negative message about the Otherworld or Afterlife is meant to be seen in the context of all the stories about the Devil, that is, as only part of the total corpus of traditional lore which the travelling people have carried down to this day. One very important point about the traveller lore in general, and most apparent in the Devil stories, is their lack of moralising. Lessons are certainly intended, but the teaching of a story can be subtle. Awareness of meanings often comes later – if you find nothing you should look to yourself!

The twelve narrations chosen for the book are published here for the first time. But other versions told by Duncan of 'The Tramp and the Farmer' and 'Jack and the Devil's Purse' have appeared in *Tocher* 3 (1971), *Tocher* 33 (1980), and *The Green Man of Knowledge* (1982). A version of 'Jack and the Devil's Gold' heard from Duncan and retold by his good friend, traveller Willie McPhee of Perth as 'The Devil's Money' is included in Sheila Douglas's collection *The King o' the Black Art* (1987).

For assistance in transcription and tape copying I should like to thank Miss Ruth Cruikshank of Tayport and Mr Fred Kent of the School of Scottish Studies, Edinburgh. I should also like to acknowledge the helpful comments of Dr Alan Bruford on an early draft of the typescript.

LINDA WILLIAMSON
Collessie, Fife
November 1988

INTRODUCTION

I. *The Coming of the Devil on Earth*

According to the mythology of the travelling people, God created Hell just the way He created heaven. It was all over a simple argument. When God created all the earth and everything else, He had many angels, people in heaven to help him. And one that He liked more than anybody else was Lucifer, He loved Lucifer. And this angel looked up to God and adored everything that He did under the sun. Anything that God would do, Lucifer was always there. He was God's right-hand man in heaven. But Lucifer had a mother, Magog, and he lived with her. Now Magog loved her son dearly, he was her only son. But they were very unhappy, especially the old mother, because Magog believed her son was more powerful than God and cleverer. She was jealous of her son's love for God.

She was always getting on to him and telling him, 'Why do you have to be at God's beck and call every moment? Why do you look up to this man and do everything for Him? Why should He be the boss, you're as good as what He is. *You* could be that person instead of Him! You're stronger than Him, you're as clever as what He is.'

And this began to penetrate Lucifer's mind. He was a clever man, he was intelligent, he had learned many things from God. So after his mother's aggravation for many nights,

1

many weeks and many months he could stand it no more. He went to God and he tellt God all this that his mother had told him.

He said to God, 'Why do I need to bow before you? Am I just something you've created that you can treat as a slave?'

And God said, 'No, you are my right-hand man. You're one of my favourites.'

Lucifer stood before God, 'Look, I'm just as powerful as you,' he said. 'I could be a king, King of the World as what you are.'

God shook his head sadly. He said to Lucifer, 'By the way you talk and the way you think, I don't think you're qualified to take my place.'

But he said, 'I'm stronger and fitter than you, I'm more powerful! I'm stronger than any animal you've ever created on the earth, this place you call earth. I'm stronger than the wildest bull you've ever created.'

And God said, 'Well, you don't look like one, but if you want to look like one . . .' And He pointed his finger like that – and Lucifer felt a shudder going through him – he looked down. There he had a cloven hoof.

And he said, 'Why don't you make me king, why don't you make me Under-king?'

And God said to him, 'You want to be Under-king? In heaven or earth?'

And Lucifer says, 'I want to be King of Earth.'

God said, 'Well, I don't think I could make you King of Earth, because I already have plans for another king for earth. But I can make you king – Under the Earth. You can rule Under the Earth for as long as you like, till the end of eternity.' And there God created Hell. He sent Lucifer as a fallen angel to Under the Earth. And, of course, when Lucifer went he took his mother with him.

2

The cavern of Hell, with a burning fire to keep him company and no friends but his mother around made Lucifer very very wicked. His name was then lost because he became the Prince of Darkness. He swore to his own mind that when anyone ever went into earth, or was buried under the ground, even though they were dead he would take them and torment them for everymore. He was *evil*. And this word became 'Devil', what he is called to this day, The Devil in Hell.

Down through the centuries people of the world have come to call the Devil by many different names. No one wants to actually say 'Devil' because the word is too evil. They refer to him using by-names instead. In Scotland he is known as 'Old Hornie' because folk believe he has horns on his head; 'Old Clootie' because he sometimes takes the place of a wreft or a spirit standing by the graveyard with a shroud over himself scaring people to death (to get their souls); 'The Blacksmith' because his place is beside his fire, and 'Old Rouchie' because of his tough character. *Cog* is the travellers' word for him, referring to his art of deception and trickery. To this day travellers believe the Devil cannot show his face in daylight. And when he comes to you he appears in the form of a black dog, a black bull, a black stallion or in the form of a tall dark man. At night Cog can take his original form, for he is natural in darkness.

According to the travellers' idea, the Devil does not exist in this world to 'get you' and punish you and torture you for doing evil things. The Devil is there to *outwit you*. The idea goes back to when he tellt God, 'I'm more clever than you.' When he was put to Hell he still maintained that. His wish was that he wanted to be King on Earth, so he comes to people on earth to show he is superior – he wants to show he is cleverer than the people God has put on earth. He gives them many chances to compete against him, 'Can you do

3

something I can't do?' If a person is clever enough to outwit the Devil then he leaves them in peace for evermore. But if they lose, their soul is lost and taken for torture in Hell. The saying, 'May the Devil walk behind ye!' means may the Devil never catch up with you, or may you always be one step ahead of him (evil) in the contest of intelligence and knowledge! When you come in contact with the Devil, and he comes to everyone, may you be cleverer than him and outdo the enemy.

II. *Hallowe'en and the Henwife*

Hallowe'en, the 31st of October, is the night the Devil gets loose. It is his special night of freedom, when he and all the imps leave Hell, come and spread out through all the country. The idea is a very pagan one and goes back thousands of years in Scotland, when tribes of people known as Celts celebrated their new year's eve on the 31st of October. All year round these people were hard working, busy like bees or ants in a hive during the summer, getting things together to see them through the winter. On the eve of the Celtic new year everything was let loose – people really did wicked things, things they would never do the rest of the year. They would exchange wives, they would get drunk, they would swear, they would curse. Nothing was sacred and no hold was barred. Every rule in the world was broken for a week or two weeks over the Hallowe'en festival. The travellers believed the Devil was in the people at that time of year; they became devils. Some would say, 'If you werena workin with the Devil you wouldna do these things.'

At the centre of the Hallowe'en festival, even today, is the idea that the Devil is not to be *clearly* seen. Children dress up and put on 'false faces' at Halloween just like the pagans did during their festival when the Devil came; he could walk among them and no-one could distinguish him from the rest.

4

In my childhood times in Argyllshire our Hallowe'en party was a wonderful night for us. We were tinkers, we'd never been invited inside the villagers' houses and never knew what it was like inside them. But all the boys and girls of the village, me and my brothers and sisters dressed ourselves up trying to prove to everyone that nobody would find out who we really were. We would get old jackets or old coats, turn them inside out, blacken wir faces with coal cinders and get some sheep's wool to make a moustache or something. We would go round all the doors, each house in turn, and knock 'chap chap'.

'Who is it?' they would say.

'Guisers, this is Hallowe'en night! Can we come in? What have you got for us?'

Oh, they'd take us into their house, and they'd give us something, a penny and a handful of nuts. But you had to sing a song!

Well, we would sing a song and then they'd say, 'Who are ye? Are ye one of Betsy's boys?' That was my mother, they knew my mother well.

'No,' we'd say, 'we're no one o' Betsy's boys.' You didna let them know who you were! But we'd tell them before we'd go on to the next house.

Then you had to duck for apples on the floor in a big bath. Sometimes you missed and yer whole head went in and it washed all the black soot off yer face. And ye were half black and half white. And then yer sheep's wool moustache if it got wet it fell off, and your disguise was nearly gone! Next you had to try and take a bite off a treacle scone hanging on a string. You couldn't use your hands and when you tried to take a bite, this scone started to waggle and it spread all over yer face. By the end of the night we each had a big pillowslip full of nuts and oranges and apples to take home, and wir faces all covered with treacle!

5

To be safe from evil and out of the Devil's reach on Hallowe'en night the travellers believed you were to *keep within the circle*. If you sat or stood within a circle at Hallowe'en time, before twelve o'clock midnight, suppose it was only a circle of people around a fire, then you were safe from all evil for the incoming year. In the olden days the crofters in the Western Isles used to bring in the ring of a cart wheel, the iron ring and place it on the floor. All visitors who came to them stood within the wheel on Hallowe'en night. There they probably had a drink and a crack and talk. Because the belief was that within the circle till after twelve o'clock evil couldna cross. It did not matter if the circle was only drawn with your finger on the earth or drawn above your door or window; but if you werena within that circle on Hallowe'en night then ye had bad luck for the whole year following. Our greeting today, 'Hello', comes from 'halloo' or 'halo' which means *circle* – have you been hallowed, have you been within the circle for the incoming year? Travellers have called Hallowe'en 'The Night of the Circle'.

The most famous story of Hallowe'en and the Devil's spirit being stopped at the *holy circle* is 'Mary MacDonald' (not included in this collection because of its length). Mary was born to a traveller couple on Hallowe'en night and she was taken away with the Devil at her birth. She lived for seven years with her parents but disappeared on her eighth birthday when the evil spirit overcame her. For one week during her seventh year she was 'past being good', and this was under the care of the henwife. The old henwife cured Mary by seating her in the middle of the circle she had drawn on her concrete floor with a lump of white fire clay. At each end of the four quadrants of the circle she put four white crosses. Then she gave Mary a drink of the water from a boiled egg, the first egg of a pullet, a young hen's first egg which has no shell, but only a skin.

6

The henwife was a person who upset the Devil more than most. She had powers and could cure people, keep them alive when the Devil might have had them otherwise. When men were sick in bed the old henwife would come in, touch them, feel their pulse and feel their forehead. And this made them feel a thousand times better. She never needed to use potions or herbs. Just being there and using her hands, like Jesus, was enough. She had natural powers. The henwife's main source was hens. She loved her hens and her ducks and her geese for they provided eggs which she sold and gave to the poor. The more she gave, the more the hens laid. And her fowl can be thought of as food from heaven, *manna* for the hungry on earth.

The Devil shook hands with the henwife in one of my stories. He'd met his match because she was not concerned with heaven or Hell. She was beyond that. The henwife had a gift of purity; she lived alone and stayed by herself. She never married and had a family, but was old and beyond the marriage circle. This virginity was the reason for her spiritual feeling towards people – she helped everyone who came to her, she never argued, she never fought – everyone was welcome. The henwife was loved and respected for her goodness. Even queens loved the henwife, and kings in power in castles appreciated her. She earned the respect and love of the people around her because she was so pure, so understanding, so clean and truthful. Today henwives may be found all around this world. And they'll never end. There will always be a henwife as long as the're a world.

The point of the Devil stories, I think, is that every person has got an evil bit in him, let it be a child to a grown man, a girl to a grown woman. But it's only at a certain time that that piece of evil will ever show itself. Lucifer was evil when he went before God and challenged Him. And God was upset. God knew that even though he was being evil there was something good in him forbyes. Because there's no such thing as an evil person through and through. Even the Devil is likeable. There's something good in every evil one and there's something evil in every good one. It's the balance between good and evil that makes for life on earth. And this earth wouldna be worth a-living on if it wasna for the Devil!

THE QUEEN AND THE DEVIL

The old queen was very sad, sad at heart because her husband the king had just died. They had reigned together for many years and she'd had a happy life. And they only had one son whom they loved dearly. They had been very well thought of in the community. The whole country had loved their king and queen, and their beautiful young son. The queen appreciated this from her people. She gave great wonderful parties every now and then to show the people that she appreciated their love. But after the king died the queen had become very sad. And her young son the prince came to see this, and he got sad too. But he had one obsession, he liked to go hunting.

And one day out on the hunt he fell from his horse. He was hurt severely. The huntsmen carried him back to the palace, they placed him on the bed and there he lay. His back was broken. The old queen was now sadder than ever. Her husband was gone, and now her son, the only being they loved together between them was very seriously ill. She sat by his bedside and she prayed and she clasped her hands, she prayed to her God and she prayed to everyone. But he got weaker and weaker . . . he finally died.

Now the queen was really very upset and sad. The thought of everything was gone. Never no more did she show her face before her people in the village. The great palace was there,

9

and all the workers in the palace did their things. But the queen just stood by herself. She walked in the garden a sad, lonely old woman. Her husband was gone, her beautiful son was gone. She had no one left in the world. No more did they have parties in the great palace. The great fêtes and the great things were gone. And the people around the country and around the palace got sadder and sadder because they were very sad for their queen.

But one day the old queen was walking in the garden admiring her flowers which she'd tended so many times before. The weeds were growing up among them, but now she had no more thought for the flowers in her garden. Then she turned round – there stood behind her this gentleman dressed in black in a long dark cloak. She said, 'Hello!'

And he said, 'Hello!'

She said, 'Where have you come from?'

'Oh,' he said, 'never mind where I come from, my dear. I've been walking here admiring you. I've been watching you for a few days, and you seem very sad.'

'Oh,' she said, 'I am very sad. Who are you?'

'Oh,' he said, 'I'm just a stranger.'

And she could see that he was dressed in black from head to foot with a long cloak touching the ground. She said, 'Where have you come from?'

'Oh,' he said, 'never mind where I've come from. I have just come to say hello. I can see you're very sad.'

She said, 'I'm very sad, of course there's sadness in my heart, because you know I have just lost my husband the king.'

And the stranger said, 'I know.' And he smiled to himself.

'And,' she said, 'I've just lost my son!'

'Well . . .' he said.

'He was hurt in a riding accident,' she said. 'I sat beside him, I prayed to my God to help him. But no-one could help him, he is gone.'

10

And the stranger said to her, 'Why are you so sad?'

'Well,' she said, 'why shouldn't I be sad? My husband is gone and my son is gone, there's nothing left for me in this world.'

'But there are many wonderful things left in the world for you, my dear,' he said 'You are not really old.'

'But,' she says, 'why should life go on for me? I wish that someone would take me away from this earth!'

He said, 'Well, maybe that could be arranged.'

She said, 'Who are you?'

He said, 'Well, I'm just a stranger. What would you give to be happy again?'

She says, 'Happy? I'll never be happy again, never again.'

'Oh yes!' he said. 'Happiness is for everyone.'

'But,' she says, 'how can I be happy? My son is gone and my husband is gone. How . . .'

He said, 'I can make you happy.'

She says, 'What are you? Are you a magician or something?'

'No, my dear, I'm not a magician,' he said, 'I'm just a friend, and a stranger.'

'Well, it's nice to be happy, but,' she said, 'where am I going to find happiness?'

He said, 'What would you give for happiness?'

She said, 'I'd give anything in this world.'

'Would you give your soul,' he said 'for happiness?'

'My soul?' she said. 'What is my soul to me, if I have one? I have prayed to my God for my son and He never helped me. If my soul is worth anything I would give it today if only I could find a little happiness!'

And the stranger said, '*Happiness you shall have!* But I will come and see you again.' And then he was gone.

The queen walked around the garden and she looked all around, she said, 'These flowers are full of weeds. The gardener has not been tending to the flowers. The trees have never been looked after!'

A great change had come over the queen. She had completely forgot about everthing but her garden. She went out and she told the workers, 'My garden's been neglected, the flowers are covered with weeds and the trees have never been pruned for months. Where are all my workers, what have you done to my garden!' And when everybody saw that the queen was worried about her garden they rushed to tidy it up, and they worked in the garden as hard as they could.

And up goes the queen to her room. She looks all around, she says, 'My room is so untidy!' There were things lying all around the floor, 'Who has done this to my place?' she said. And the queen called for all her maids at hand, 'Get my room tidied up at once!'

They tidied up her room. They talked to each other and said, 'What has come over our queen? Something terrible has happened. She is smiling, she is happy once again.'

So the queen walks out to the front of the palace, and it was dreich and barren, everything looked so dark and grey. She stood over the balcony and she said, 'Where are all my people? Where are all my friends? Why is everyone so sad?'

Everyone looked all around and said, 'A strangeness has come over the queen.'

She said, 'Why is everyone so sad? Where's the party? Where are all my friends? Where are all the guests? Where are all the people?' There was no one. The queen sent word all around the palace, 'Get my people to come before me!' she said 'Let's have fun. Let's have a party! Let's have a fête! Let's have everything we used to have!'

So word spread around the palace that once again 'the queen was happy'. And they started and they set a royal fête where everyone came all around to see the queen once more.

They came from far and wide, they* came knights from far off, they came lairds and dukes and people from the village and they were having a great party in front of the palace. An' in amongst them walked the queen saying 'hello' to everyone an' bowing to everyone. Everyone was happy. They had drinking and fêtes and fighting and battles and they had everything – life once again was back to normal. There were jugglers, there were singers, everyone was happy, having great fun! When lo and behold at that very moment in amongst everyone walked this tall dark stranger with a long black cloak. And there sat the queen up on her bench before everyone watching everyone enjoying theirself.

When he walked up to the queen and said, 'Hello, my dear! Sppst,' he spat and *flame* came from his mouth.

And the queen stood back, she said, 'Who are you?'

He said, 'Who am I? You are bound to recognise me! I have come to see you. You gave me your promise . . . now are you happy?'

'Happy?' she said. 'I'm happier than anyone in the world, I'm happy!'

'Well,' he said, 'I gave you the happiness. Now I have come for you. You must come with me,' and he 'sppst' – spat again and *flames* spat from his mouth.

The queen said, 'Look . . .'

He said, 'Do you remember when I met you in the garden? When you wanted happiness? And you promised me you would give your soul, everything I wanted to give you happiness?'

She said, 'Yes.'

'Well,' he said, 'I gave you happiness. Are you happy?'

'Of course,' she said. 'I'm happy.'

'Don't you have everything you had before?' he said. 'And I provided it for you. Now, you must come with me.'

* they – there

13

She says, 'No! I can't come with you. I am too happy.'

But he said, 'You promised me!'

She said, 'Guards! Arrest this man!' And the guards drew back their bows and arrows to arrest him.

He held out his hand like that – from every finger came the heads of ten snakes with their beady eyes glaring and their fangs and their tongues going out and in, their forked tongues going out and in. And he said, 'Well, let them come to me, my dear!' He held his hands and the tongues of the snakes with the beady eyes . . .

'Use your spears! Use your arrows!' she said. And they fired! They hit his chest and the spears stotted off like lumps of steel and fell on the ground.

And he walked among them with his fingers sticking out. And the heads of the snakes – the people cringed in terror back from him. He followed them back, he raised his fingers with these ten snakes, their beady eyes and their tongues in front of them. And the queen sat in terror. Everyone backed away. And then he went up to the queen and he closed his fingers, the snakes were gone. 'Now,' he said, 'my dear, it is time for you to come with me.'

She says, 'No! You are the Devil!'

'Of course,' he said, 'I am the Devil.'

'Well,' she said, 'if you're the Devil I've heard many stories of you. You always give people a chance.'

He said, 'You prayed to your God, didn't you?'

'I prayed to my God,' she said, 'to save my son, but he never saved my son.'

'Well,' he said, 'you asked me to make you happy and I made you happy. Now you have everything you want and you gave me your promise.'

She says, 'Please, if you are the Devil, an' the stories I've heard about you . . . please give me one more chance. One more chance I beg of you!'

And the Devil said, 'Of course, I always give people a chance. I'll be back. In three weeks' time, my dear, on condition that *you can do something that I can't do, and failing that you shall come with me!*' And then in a *flash* he was gone.

The queen was upset. She knew she was in touch with the Devil. The Devil had taken over her soul. She told everyone around the palace what was going to happen – the Devil was coming for her in three weeks' time. Could she do something that the Devil could not do? They came from all parts of the earth, from all parts of her kingdom, telling her this and telling her that, things that she could do to cheat the Devil. The queen listened to them, but one by one all the things they knew, she knew the Devil could compete against anything she heard, till she was in tears and worried that the Devil was coming for her. When up to her palace came an old shepherd with a little bag on his back and a little bag under his arm with a long grey beard and a ragged coat. He stepped up the stairs.

He was stopped immediately by the guards and they said, 'Where are you going, old man?'

'Well,' he said, 'I am just an old shepherd and I have come to help the queen.'

So everybody was interested. Any who could give help to the queen would be acceptable. So the old shepherd was led up to the queen's chamber, and there sat the queen in great grief knowing that within a week the Devil was coming to take her.

And the old shepherd stepped up and said, 'Your Majesty, I am believing you have been in touch with the Devil, an' he has challenged you to a great duel, that you could do something that he could not do.

She said, 'Of course, you have heard, my friend.'

'Well' he said, 'I am just an old shepherd, my dear, My Majesty, and I have come to help you.'

15

She said, 'No one can help me. I've heard many things from all of my subjects all over the land, and nothing that they've said can help me.'

'But,' he said, 'my dear, I can help you.' And from under his arm he took a very small sheepskin bag, and he held it up to her. He said to her, 'In this little bag, my dear, is something that will help you.'

And the queen took it, a small sheepskin bag. She shaked it, it was full of water. She said to him, 'And what can I do with this, old shepherd?'

He said, 'All you can do with it, my dear, is take it and put it in two halfs between two little measures. And wait till the Devil comes back to you again. Ask him to take one drink, and you take the other.'

So the queen thanked the old shepherd and she said, 'If this works, my friend, I will repay you for everything you have done for me. You are only a shepherd, but if this works for me you will never be a shepherd again.'

'Don't worry,' says the old man, 'don't worry about it. Just forget it. But remember what I told you.'

So the old shepherd went on his way, and the queen stood with the little bag. She then kept it within her bedroom, she pressed it to her heart and she blessed it. And soon the time passed. It was time for the Devil to return once again. She went into the room and she took two little silver glasses, silver drinking glasses, and she halved the water of the little bag in two. She placed them on the table and there she waited. She sat and she waited and soon it was twelve o'clock on the very day that the Devil said he was coming back.

Then there was a *flash* in the room! There he stood once again with his long dark cloak beside her. He said 'My dear, I have come back.'

'Oh yes,' she said, 'I know you've come back.'

He said, 'Do you remember what I told you?'

16

She said 'Yes, I have.'

'Now,' he said, 'you asked for a second chance and I gave it to you. Now can you do something I can't do?'

And she said, 'Well I think I can.' And she picked up the glasses, the little silver drinking glasses. She passed one to him and she said, 'You drink that one and I'll drink the other.' The queen lifted it up and she drank it down, and placed the glass on the table. 'Now,' she said, 'Devil, you drink the other half.'

And the Devil put it to his mouth and he tasted it, 'sppst!' He spat it out! 'Queen, there's no-one can make the Devil drink Holy Water!' he said. And that is the end of my story.

THE DEVIL'S COAT

There was once this old traveller man and his wife. They
travelled, walking mostly round Perthshire. Their two children
had grown up and left them, and got married. But this old
man and his old wife always came back to the same wee place
every winter to stay. And they camped in this wee wood by
the side of the road. Now he was a very nice easy-going man
and so was the woman. The folk of the district knew them
very well and respected them for what they were. So this year
the old man and woman had been away all summer
wandering here and there, and the wife had sold stuff from
her basket, he'd made baskets and tinware. They'd made
their way back once more to their winter camping place.

The old wife was hawking the houses with her basket round
the doors that she knew and everybody welcomed her, glad to
see her back again. Now this man was an awful nice old man,
he was really good. And his old wife really thought the world
of him. At the week-end on a Saturday he would walk to the
nearby village to the wee bar and have a couple pints of beer.
His old wife would sit and do something at home at the camp till
he came back. But they'd only been at this place for about a
week when it came Saturday, and it landed on Hallowe'en night.

'Maggie,' he said to her, 'I think I'll dander awa along the
length o' the town to the pub and hae a couple o' pints, pass
the night awa.'

'Well,' she said, 'John, as long as ye dinna be too late. Because I'm kind o' feart when it gets dark at night-time to sit here myself, and especially when it's Hallowe'en. And it bein Hallowe'en night ye ken the Devil's loosed, supposed tae be on Hallowe'en night!'

'You and your devil,' the old man says, 'ye're awfa superstitious. Ye ken fine the're no such a thing as the devil!'

'Well never mind,' she says, 'I've got my beliefs and you've got yours. But try and get hame as soon as ye can.'

'All right,'says the old man, 'I'll no wait long. I havena much money to spend, a couple o' shillings.' So he says 'cheerio' to his old wife and away he goes.

Now from where they stayed in this wee wood at the roadside he had about a mile to go. But before he came to the wee village there was a burn, and a bad bend and a bridge to cross. So the old man lighted his pipe and walked away to the village and landed at the pub. He spent his couple o' bob and had a few pints to himself. But he met in with two or three other folk he had known, country folk from about the district that he used to work for, and they kept him later than he really thought it was. But it must have been near closing time – he clean forgot about his old wife – it was near about half past ten at night when he finally left the pub. And he wasn't really drunk.

So he dandered home till he came to the bridge, and it was a dark dark night. Barely a star shining. Just as he came to the bridge before the bad bend he said, 'Everybody says this bridge is haunted, haunted by the Devil. But I dinnae believe in nae devils!' But just when he came over the bridge and round the bend he seen this thing lying across the middle o' the road in front o' him. 'God bless me,' said the man, 'somebody must be drunk and fell in the road.' But he came up closer to it . . . he seen it was a coat. And the old man picked it up, 'I'll carry it on to the camp,' he said. 'Maybe

20

somebody had dropped it, maybe the laird or some o' the gamekeepers goin hame from the pub must hae dropped it. But it's a good coat,' that he could see. So he travelled on. Home he came. And he had a wee barrikit built up and his wee lamp, the cruisie was going.

The old woman says to him, 'You're kind o' late, where were ye?'

'Ach,' he said, 'Maggie, I met two or three folk in the pub, men I used to work for, do wee bits o' jobs for and they kept me crackin. I'm sorry for bein late.'

'Aye,' she said, 'it's all right yinst you're back. Were ye no feart to come ower that brig?'

'What am I going to be feart of?' he said.

She says, 'Feart o' Cog, the Devil! This is Hallowe'en night.'

'Ach, you and your superstition,' he said.

She says, 'What's that you've got there?'

He said, 'A coat I found on the brig.'

'Oh,' she said, 'a coat . . . hmm. Let me look at it.' And the old woman looked at it. 'Well,' she said, 'John, I've seen many's a coat, but that's the prettiest coat I've ever seen in my life!' It was black, it had black velvet neck, velvet sleeves and velvet pockets. And black shiny buttons, four black shiny buttons. She said, 'It's a beautiful coat. But I'll tell ye, it must hae fell off some o' the coaches goin to the town. It must be some high-up body's coat that, because that's nae poor man's coat.'

'Well, I've been lookin for a coat like this all my days,' he said.

She says, 'Ye're no goin to keep it are ye?'

'Oh aye, I'm goin to keep it, I'm goin to keep it all right,' he said. 'I've always wanted a coat like this. And naebody'll ever ken I've got it, I'm keepin it!'

'Well,' she says, 'Ye might be keepin it, John, but what if somebody comes lookin for it?'

21

'I'll say I never seen nae coat on the road,' he said. 'I want it and I'm goin to keep it!'

'Oh well,' she says, 'please yersel!'

So the old man has had his tea. He sat cracking to his old wife a wee while and sat telling her about the folk he met in the pub and that. He went to bed. It was a cold night, cold frosty night. 'Maggie,' he said, 'I'm goin to fling that coat ower the top of the bed to keep us warm.'

'Ah well,' she says, 'it'll ay help, it's a cold night.'

So after the old man and the old woman had made their bed the old man flung the coat over the top of them. But he was lying smoking for a wee while his pipe and the old man rose to go outside. He was a good wee while out, and all in a minute he heard a scream. He ran back, and this was the old woman she's sitting and shaking with fright! 'God bless us, woman,' he said, 'What's wrong wi ye?'

'Dinna speak to me – it's that coat!' she said.

'Aye, coat,' he said, 'the're nothin wrong wi the coat!'

'No,' she said, 'maybe you dinna ken the're nothin wrong with it. These four buttons that's on that coat, when you were out they turned into four eyes and they were shinin at me and winkin at me!'

'Ah, ye must hae fell asleep while I was outside doin a wee job to myself,' he said.

'No,' she said, 'Johnnie, no, I never fell asleep. I'm tellin you, that coat's haunted – that's *the Devil's coat* frae the haunted brig!'

'Na,' he said, 'woman, you ought to have more sense than that.' But the old man laid down again. He happed the coat back over him. But during the night he turned to the old woman, said, 'Maggie, do you no feel it's awfa warm?'

'Aye,' she said, 'it's awfa warm.'

'God bless us,' he said, 'the sweat's breakin off me and it's a cold night like this!'

'I tellt ye,' she said, 'it's that *coat.*'

'Aye,' he said, 'the coat! Lie down and hap yourself and pull the coat up!' But the old man tossed and turned and he moaned all night. And he wakened up, the sweat was lashing off him and so was his old woman. 'Maggie,' he said, 'it's an awfa warm night!'

She said 'It's no warm – it's a frosty winter's night!'

'Well,' he said, 'lie back down!' Now the old man began to get kind o' umperant* and cheeky to the old woman. Every word the woman said he began to lose his temper. Now he never was like this to the old woman before. But during the night he said, 'Woman, would ye get off the top o' me!'

She says, 'I'm no near ye.'

He said, You were lying on top o' me a minute ago, I felt the weight o' you on top o' me!'

She says, 'No!' And the old woman rose up, she was wet with sweat and so was he. She said, 'It's that *coat!*'

'God curse you and the coat!' he said. And he catcht the coat and he flung it at the foot o' the bed. And it lay down at the foot o' the bed. The old man fell asleep and his old wife. And he wakened up, he was frozen, cold as could be. 'God bless us,' he said, it's awfa cold. I'm frozen.'

She said, 'You were sweatin a minute ago an complainin about somebody lyin a-top o' you.'

And he started to the old woman, he gave the woman the most cheek and umperance in the world. And he was going to hit her, 'Only for you,' he said, 'I could hae my coat ower the top o' me! You and this silly mental carry-on o' ye – you and your mad beliefs!'

'Well, you'll no believe it, it's that *coat!* The best thing ye can do,' she said, 'get rid o' it, or I'm no goin to bide in the camp wi ye wi it nae mair!'

* umperant – impudent

23

He said,'I'm keepin the coat and you shut up!' He'd never said that to his old wife before in his life.

But the next morning the old woman got up, kindled the fire and made a wee cup o' tea. She offered the old man a cup o' tea.

'Leave it down there, I'll get it when I'm ready!' he said.

The woman looked at him. He never was like that with her before. But the more the week passed . . . the old woman went away and done a bit hawking, came back. But no, the fire was out, the old man was sitting at the fire, he'd hardly speak to her and snapped at every word she said to him.

'John,' she said, 'what's comin ower you?'

He said, 'The're nothing coming over me, nothing at all.'

She said, 'Ye're demented some way.'

He said, 'I'm no demented.'

She said, 'Did ye look . . . were there anything in the pockets o' that coat you found in the road?'

'Aye,' he said, 'there were something in one pocket. But you're no gettin it, I'm keepin it!'

She says, 'What was it?'

He said, 'A sixpence, a silver sixpence. And I'm keepin it. You're no gettin it, dinna ask it!'

'Ah well,' says the old woman, 'I canna dae nothin with you. The best thing ye can dae is go back and put that coat where you got it.'

'No,' he says, 'I'm no puttin the coat where I got it. I'm goin to keep it, suppose it's the Devil's coat I'm keepin it!'

'Oh well,' she said, 'it's up to yourself.'

But the days passed by and the old man got worse every day. He got so that the old woman couldn't put up with him. Her life was greetin terrible* with him for nearly a week. The old man was demented and the old woman couldn't get a

* greetin terrible – utterly miserable

24

minute's peace with him. Every night . . . the coat over him, the coat off him, the coat over him, the coat off him. And the old woman wouldna bide in the tent with the coat for God!

But one day she says to herself, 'I canna take this nae longer. Either he goes or I go. If the coat disna go, I'll go,' she tellt the old man.

'You can go if you want,' he said, 'but I'm keepin the coat.'

'Oh well,' she said . . . the woman lifted her wee basket and away she went. She wandered away down to an old woman she knew, an old henwife who kept hens on a wee croft.

Out comes the woman, 'Oh, it's yourself, Maggie,' she says.

'Aye.'

'Ye back for the winter?'

'Aye, I'm back for the winter.'

'Well, ye're just in time. I was cleaning up and haein a wee cup o' tea. Come on in and hae a wee cup o' tea wi me,' she said. So this old hen woman liked old Maggie awful much. She said, 'I'll hae a look for some stuff to ye afterward.' The old woman made her a cup o' tea and gave her scones and cheese. 'Oh, by the way,' she says, 'how is old John gettin on? Is he keepin all right?'

'No,' says Maggie, 'he's no keepin all right, to tell ye the truth. There's something far wrong with him.'

'Oh, God bless me,' says the old henwife, 'he's no ill is he?'

'No,' says the old woman, 'he's no ill, no ill nae way . . . he's worse than ill – he's demented! And bad and wicked.'

'Well,' says the old henwife, 'it's a droll thing. I've kent old John for many's a year. He used to come here and dig my garden and cut sticks for me, do a wee bit job for me. And the're no a nicer old man that ever walked the country. Everybody in the district has got a great name about him.'

'Well,' she says, 'he's a changed man today. Ever since he found that *coat*.'

25

'What coat?' says the old henwife.

So the old woman up and tellt her the story.

'Oh . . .' she said, 'did he look the pockets out?'

'Aye,' she said, 'he looked the pockets out.'

She said, 'What was in the pocket o' the coat?'

She said, 'A sixpence.'

'Ah,' the old woman said , 'a sixpence, aye . . . What kind o' coat was it?'

She tellt her, 'Long and black, velvet neck, velvet pockets and four black-horned shiny buttons. And to mak it worse, the night he brung it back old John went outside for a wee walk to hisself, an' I looked. As low as my mother,' she says to the old woman, 'I'll no tell you a lie, but I could swear on the Bible these four buttons turned into four eyes and they were winkin and blazin at me!'

'God bless me,' says the old woman, 'where did he get it?'

She says, 'He found it on the bridge, the haunted bridge goin to the village.'

'Oh aye,' said the old woman, 'hmmm. Well, I'll tell ye, the morn's Sunday and I'm goin to the church to the village. Would it be all right if I take a wee walk in and see you on the road past?'

'I wish to God you would, and try and talk some sense into him,' she says.

'I'll drop in and hae a wee crack to old John on the road past,' she says, 'when I'm comin goin to the church.'

'All right,' says the old woman.

So she gave the old traveller woman eggs and butter and a can o' milk and everything she needed. She bade her 'farewell' and away went Maggie home to the camp.

When she came home the old man's sitting cross-legged with the coat beside him. He wouldn't hardly speak to her. No fire, his face no washed or nothing. And his two eyes were rolling in his head. The old woman kindled the fire and made him some tea. She offered . . .

'No,' he said, 'I'm no wantin nothing fae ye. Don't want nothing fae ye, not nothing at all!'

'God bless me, John,' she said, 'that's no a way to carry-on. What's wrong wi ye?'

He said, 'There's nothing wrong wi me. What's wrong with you?'

'Oh,' she said, 'the're nothing wrong with me.'

But anyway, that night again the old woman wouldn't let him put the coat over the bed. And they argued all night about it. The old man gave in at last, he flung it at the foot o' the bed.

But next morning the old woman got up again, made a cup o' tea. The old man took a cup o' tea, nothing else, hardly speaking, just snapping at every word she spoke to him. 'Well,' she said, 'John, there's somethin far wrong with you, since ever you found that coat. As low as my father, that is *the Devil's coat!*'

'I'm no carin,' he said, 's'pose it's the Devil's father's coat, I'm keepin it!'

'Well,' she said, 'if you keep it, you canna keep me!'

'Well,' he said, 'if it comes to the choice, you ken where your family is. You can go and stay with them, I'll stay wi my coat.'

The old woman couldn't see what to do with him. But they were still arguing away when up comes the old henwife with her wee hat and coat on and her handbag in one hand, her prayer book and Bible in below her oxter. It was only two steps off the road to the wood where the old man and woman were staying.

The old woman stepped in, she said 'Hello, Maggie, how are ye?'

'Oh,' she said, 'hello!'

She spoke to old John, 'Hello, John, how are ye?'

'Oh,' he says, 'I'm no so bad, I'm no any better wi you askin anyway! Ye'll be up here for me to do some mair cheap work for ye – work for you for nothin!'

'No,' she says, 'John, I'm no up tae gie ye mair work for nothing.' The old woman was dubious right away, the old man was never like this before. 'To tell ye the truth, John, I'm a bit worried,' she says. 'Maggie was down crackin to me yesterday and she tellt me about the coat you found at the bridge.'

He said, 'She had nae right tellin ye about the coat. I warned her not to tell naebody about it.'

'Well,' she said, 'John, I want to see it.'

He said, 'Do you want to – do ye ken somebody belongin to it?'

'No,' she said, 'I dinna ken naebody belongin to it. But I want to see it.'

So the old man went out and he got the coat, he held it up.

The old woman came up close to him, she says, 'Hold that up by the neck!' He held it up, she looked it up and down. She looked at it a long long while. She could fair see it was just sleek and shining like sealskin. She says, 'John, what did you do with the sixpence you got in the pocket o' it?'

'Oh,' he says, 'did that old bitch o' mine tell ye that too? Well, I've got it in my pocket and I'm keepin it.'

She says, 'John, I want ye to do somethin for me.'

He says, 'What is it?'

She says, 'I want you to put that sixpence back in the pocket and hold up the coat!'

The old man looked at her for a long while. But something came over him when he looked at the old woman . . . the way the old woman looked at him. And he got kind o' calm and quiet. He held up the coat by the neck, he dropped the sixpence in the coat pocket. The old man opened the other pocket and the old woman dropped in the Bible.

28

Well, when she dropped the Bible into that coat pocket the coat jumped about ten feet in the air! And the arms started to flap, and it was up and down and running about same as it was demented. Till the old woman said to old John, 'Run and catch it, stand on it!' The old man got a terrible fright and the old woman got a terrible fright. The old man was shaking like the leaf o' a tree and so was the old woman. The old man began to realise now there was something far wrong with this coat.

So the old man stood on it with his feet. And the old woman leaned down, she put her hand in the pocket and took the Bible out. 'Now, John,' she said, 'I'll tell ye, I'm goin to the church. You walk along with me to the bridge. Take that coat wi ye.'

Old Maggie said, 'I'm no bidin here mysel. I'll walk wi yese.'

So the three o' them walked along to the bridge, and the old woman said, 'Where did ye find the coat?'

He says, 'I found it just there, that bad bend, the dark corner at the bridge, it was lyin across the road.'

So the old woman says, 'Roll it up in a knot!' And the old man rolled it up like that. 'Now,' she says, 'throw it over the bridge!' And the old woman opened the Bible and she said, 'God bless us all!' while the old man flung the coat over the bridge. When it hit the water it went in a *blaze o' fire* and disappeared!

The old man looked, 'God bless me,' he said to the old woman, 'it definitely was *the Devil's coat*.'

So the old henwife said, 'Aye, John that was *the Devil's coat*, that was lost when he came here on Halloween night. But it never was *lost*, it was left specially for you! If you'd hae spent that sixpence, you'd hae been with the Devil.'

'Well,' he said to the old woman, 'thank God you saved me.'

And the old man put his arm round his old wife and the two o' them walked home. The old man said to her, 'Look, as long as I live, Maggie, never again will I cross that brig at night-time.' And from that day on the old man never crossed that bridge again till whatever day he died. He was the nicest old man to his old wife in the world, and life went on as if nothing ever had happened! And that's the last o' my wee story.

JACK AND THE SEA WITCH

Once upon a time Jack lived with his mother in a wee cottage by the shore. His father had died when he was young and he was reared by his mother. And further along the shore lived his mother's old sister, his old auntie, in another house. Jack visited her frequently from time to time when he was a boy, and his auntie loved him as much as his mother did. But all Jack's time he spent it on the beach, on the shores hunting the rocks and cliffs and fishing and doing everything under the sun, doing an odd bit job here and there to help his mother. And that's the way he grew up till he came to be a young man. His mother and his auntie adored him because he was such a good laddie. Till one day he came home and he was sitting after his supper, sitting very quiet.

He says, 'Mother . . .'

She says, 'What is it, Jack?'

He said, 'How can you catch a mermaid?'

'Laddie,' she said, 'you canna catch a mermaid. Mermaids disna exist, they only exist in folk's minds. Sailors tell stories o' seein mermaids, but it's no really a *mermaid*.'

He says, 'Mother, I've seen a real mermaid. And I've been watchin her now for months. I've fallen in love wi her, and I want to catch her.'

'Ach, laddie,' she says, 'you've been dreamin! You fell

31

asleep along the shore some place, the way you always
wander on them rocks and you've dreamed it.'

'No, Mother,' he said, 'I never dreamed it.'

'Well I dinna ken,' she says, 'they tell so many tales about
folk catchin mermaids. They say you can catch them and you
tak off their tail and you can hide their tail or do whatever
you can, but I dinna ken very much about it. But I'll tell ye,
gang along to yer auntie and tak some bits o' messages down
to her, I was going to send you down to her anyway. She's older
than me and she kens an awfa lot mair than me about these
sorts o' things. She's been all her days at the sea, and if there's
anybody in the world can tell ye about mermaids and put that
silly notion out o' yer head maybe she'll help ye a wee bit.'

'Okay, Mother,' he says. And she could see by it he was
kind o' worried.

So she packs a wee basket with bits o' things for her old
sister, who was getting up in years, maybe in her seventies,
gives them to Jack and Jack goes along the shore, his path to
his auntie's. And when she got him away, 'That silly laddie o'
mine,' she says to herself. 'God knows, maybe he did see a
mermaid. Ach, it's hard to believe, too, that there is such a
thing as a mermaid. I heard his father, and a good sailor he
was at one time, away for years, sayin that many's a man had
seen a mermaid, and they decoyed sailors awa. But ach, I
dinna ken. Anyway he'll forget it soon.'

But away Jack goes, travels along the beach to his old
auntie's. The old woman stayed on the shore and kept ducks,
looked after and kept nothing but ducks. Up he goes. His old
auntie was pottering about the house when he landed.

'Oh it's yersel, Jack,' she said, 'how's yer mother keeping?'

'No bad, auntie,' he said. 'There's two-three bits o' things
she sent down to ye.'

'Aye, put them in there. And I'll come in and mak ye a wee
mouthful o' tea,' she said.

So Jack goes in, sits down at the fireside . . . and then puts a fire on for his auntie. She comes in, mutch on her head and a long frock on her. She sits down at the fireside. She gives him something to eat. 'Ye ken, I'm no very hungry, auntie,' he said.

She says, 'Jack, I ken you better than that, son. What's bothering ye?'

'Ach well, auntie, tell ye the truth,' he said, 'ye'll maybe no believe me what I'm goin to tell ye, but . . . I want to catch a mermaid.'

'What?' she said. 'Laddie, do ye ken what ye're sayin?'

'Aye,' he said, 'auntie, I want to catch a mermaid and I dinna ken how to catch her.'

The old woman sat for a long long while, she thought. She said, 'Laddie, did ye see a mermaid?'

'Aye, auntie, I've seen a mermaid,' he said. 'I've been seein her now for months, all summer. And she comes into this wee narrow lagoon, but when I go down she escapes back through it and I've nae way in the world to catch her.'

She says, 'Laddie, ye ken, I half believe ye and I dinna believe ye.'

'But auntie,' he says, 'between me and my father in the grave, I'm tellin ye the truth! I've seen a mermaid.'

She says, 'Laddie, you've got to be careful what you catch in the seas round about here. There's many's and many a thing that naebody kens that I ken. The're many's a droll thing can be catcht in the sea! Well, if your mind's made up, there's only one way to catch a mermaid . . . You'll have to go and search for Blind Rory the Netmaker. And he'll mak ye a net to catch a mermaid if it's a mermaid you want. But I'm telling ye, laddie, for yer ain sake, ye're better to leave well alone! Oh, I've heard stories o' men catchin mermaids and hidin their tails and doin all sorts o' things, but never nae good come out o' it. It's ay bad luck! Oh, they're bonnie

things when you see them, but they can also be a sheer lot o'
trouble to you.'

'Auntie, I want to catch a mermaid!' he said. 'I've seen her,
I love her and I want her!'

'Well,' said the old auntie, 'let you be your own judge. You
go and search out Blind Rory.'

'But,' he said, 'where am I goin to find Blind Rory?'

'Well,' she said, 'the last I heard o' him, he stays many
many miles awa fae here on the beach, him and his grand-
daughter. And he maks nets. He's the man to see! I dinna ken
if he'll gie ye a net or no, or mak ye yin, or what ye can do.
But for yer ain mind and for yer ain sense o' peace or justice
. . . go back and tell yer mother what I tellt ye, to forget the
whole thing! And leave well alone.'

'No, auntie,' he said. 'There'll be nae peace for me till I
catch a mermaid.'

'Well, well,' she said, 'son, please yersel. But I'm only
advisin ye . . .'

'I ken ye mean well, auntie,' he said, 'but it's gotten wi me
that I get nae peace o' mind till I catch this mermaid.'

'But,' she says, 'son, what are ye goin to do with a mermaid
after ye catch it?'

He says, 'Auntie, she's a young woman, the bonniest young
woman I've ever seen in my life. And all she's got is a fish's
tail – the rest o' her is perfect.'

'Ah,' she said, 'I ken, I heard my great-granny, your great-
great-granny tellin me stories when I was a wee infant years
ago that there were yin man that catcht a mermaid wonst,
and he was a sair punished man. So I'm advisin ye, Jack, for
yer ain good to go back to yer mother and forget all about it!'

'No,' he said, 'auntie! I'm no goin to forget all about it.'

'Oh well,' she says, 'please yersel. Anyway, the're a couple
o' dozen o' duck eggs, tak them up to yer mother when ye go
back. And go and please yersel. Ye're a young man, ye're

twenty years of age and there's nae use o' me tellin ye
anything. Ye canna put an old head on young shoulders, so
you do what ye want to do and come back and tell me how
you got on. And if there's any help that I can gie ye, always
remember I'm always here!'

'Right, auntie,' he said. He bade her 'farewell' and away
he went. He travelled back, back home, and up to his
mother. Mother was in the house.

'Well, Jack,' she said, 'ye're hame.'

'Aye, Mother,' he said, 'I'm hame.'

'How did ye get on?' she said. 'Did ye see yer Auntie
Maggie?'

'Aye,' he said, 'I seen her.'

'And what did she tell ye? she said. 'Did she knock some
sense into yer head?'

'No, Mother, she never knocked nae sense into my head or
she never knocked nane out o' it. She tellt me a lot o' things,
but . . . she tellt me, Mother, to gang and seek out Blind
Rory.'

'Aha,' says his mother, 'that's a job alane – seekin out
Blind Rory the Netmaker! Some folk says he works with the
Devil.'

'Well,' he said, 'If he works with the Devil surely he can mak
me a net, I'll pay him for it. I've a few shillings in my pocket.'

'Well look, Jack,' she says, 'son, you're the only son I've
got. And since your father dee'd you're the only help I've
ever had, and I dinna want to see naethin comin ower ye. I
couldna tak it if onything happened to ye. But if ye want to go
and seek out Blind Rory ye'll have to travel into the next
town and through that to the next town, fifty odd miles awa
fae here, places I've never been in my life.' But anyway, the
last I heard, my old sister tellin that some wanderin sailor
tellt her, that Blind Rory stays in some kind of cave him and
his grand-daughter near some town.'

'Well, well, Mother,' he says, 'I'll no get nae peace o' mind till I go and find out for mysel.'

So next morning Jack gets up early. His mother packs him a wee bundle of whatever he needed to carry him along the road, his coat and his bit o' meat in a bundle for himself. And he flung it on his back and away he goes. On he travels, he travels and he travels and on and on and on. Comes night-time he kindles a wee fire, makes himself a bite to eat and lies down to sleep at the back of a tree. He does the same the next day and the next day till he comes to the first town. And by good luck it was a fishing town. Jack never was here before, the place was all strange to him. And he sees an old man sitting on a summer-seat, a seat at the side o' the shore. He walks up to the old man.

'Excuse me, old man,' he said, 'I'm lookin for a man they cry Blind Rory the Netmaker. He's supposed to be no far fae here.'

The old man took a good look at him, scratched his head. 'Ah, laddie, laddie,' he said, 'what are ye wantin Blind Rory for? I thought the likes o' you would hae mair sense to keep awa fae folk like that! Do ye no ken the legend that Blind Rory works with the Devil? All these shipwrecked sailors and things that's done in the sea, they say Blind Rory's the cause o' it. He wrecks boats and things for the sake o' gettin the stuff off them when they come in wi the tide.'

'Ach,' says Jack, 'I dinna believe them stories. I'll see for mysel.'

'Well, I'll tell ye,' says the old man, 'I'm an old sailor mysel. And ye'll gang on twenty-five mile to the next town, and when ye get there go down to the beach. And right close to the waterside ye'll come to a wee white house, and that's my old brother. Tell him I sent ye and he'll help ye!'

'Good,' says Jack, and he bade the old man 'farewell'. Away goes Jack and he travels and he travels and he travels on. He comes to the town and walks through the town, walks along the beach and he comes to the wee white house. He walks round to the front o' the house and the're an old bended man with a long grey beard sawing sticks at the front o' the house. 'Hello!' says Jack.

'Hello!' says the old man. 'What can I do for ye?'

'Well,' says Jack, 'to tell ye the truth I've come from the neighbouring town and I met an old man who said he was your brother.'

'Oh aye,' he said, 'my old brother, oh aye. I haena seen him for years. But anyway, what have ye come to see me about?'

'Well,' he said, 'to tell ye the truth, old man, I've come to see ye could you help me?'

'Ah well,' says the old man, 'by the looks o' you, a young strong powerful man like you, ye dinna need nae help fae the likes o' me!'

'Ah but,' says Jack, 'the kind o' help I want I canna do it for mysel. I want to ken where's Blind Rory!'

'Blind Rory?' says the old man. 'What are you wantin him for? Ye ken it's even bad luck to speak about Blind Rory in this place never mind gang and see him!'

He says, 'I want him to mak me a net.'

'Oh,' says the old man, 'he'll mak ye a net. He'll mak ye a net, but it's what ye get in the net after ye get it! I ken many stories about folk that bought nets fae him here and . . . droll droll things happen to them. His nets is good, but it's what you catch in them . . .'

'Well, that's what I want,' says Jack. 'I want a net to catch a mermaid!'

The old man says, 'What age are ye?'

He says, 'I'm twenty.'

'Oh ye're twenty. What age do you think I am?' the old man says to him.

37

'Ah,' Jack says, 'Ye're an old man about sixty or seventy.'

Old man says; 'I'm ninety! And I've seen an awfa lot o' mair years than you. And I'm telling ye, don't ever try and catch a mermaid! Because it's bad luck. Ye're too young to get bad luck at yer time o' life.'

Jack says, 'Look, old man, are ye goin to tell me or are you no goin to tell me where can I find Blind Rory? I'm no wanting nae mair o' yer stories. I'm sick with you and your brother and my mother and my auntie all tellin me the same thing! Can you no let me think mysel what to do for a while?'

'Well,' says the old man, 'you have it your way. Go along that beach there and go round the first big clift face to the second clift face, and then the third clift face you'll come to a bay. And somewhere in that bay – there's nae road to it – ye'll find a cave, and in that cave is Blind Rory with his grand-daughter.'

'Right,' says Jack.

'But I'm tellin ye, it's a long long way and it's a sheer clift all the way, so you'd better watch yerself!'

'I'll watch mysel,' says Jack.

He goes back to the town and he buys two-three messages to help him on his way, and away he goes. He wanders on and he wanders on up this wee clift and down this wee clift, round this wee bay and through this wee path. He wanders here and wanders there till he goes round the first clift, round the second clift, round the third clift right down till he comes to the third bay, till he's that tired he has to sit down on the sand with his back against a rock. And he must have been sitting for about an hour when he sees this bonnie red-headed lassie with her hair down her back running down along the beach. Jack saw her and he ran after her.

When she saw him coming she tried to make off, but he was faster than her and he catcht up with her. She turned round to him and she was like a wildcat. She said, 'What do you

38

want off me, leave me alone! Youse folk . . . we keep to wirsel, we don't want –'

'Wait, wait, wait, lassie,' he said, 'wait! I dinna want to do ye nae harm. I'm no here to touch ye.'

'Well,' she said, 'what do you want off me? I never interfere with nobody in this world, so leave us alone.'

He said, 'I want to see your grandfather.'

The lassie stopped. She said, 'What do you want to see my grandfather for?'

He said, 'I want to get a net fae him.'

'Oh aye! Well, if that's all ye want, you better come wi me.' So the lassie walked along the shore and he followed her up this path to this clift face. She said, 'Stand there!' An opening hung with canvas in the face of the clift.

Jack must have stood for about five minutes and he heard arguing and chatting and speaking inside this big monster cave. He could hear the voices echoing away back into it. But anyway, the lassie came out.

She says, 'Ye can come in seeing you've come this distance.'

In goes Jack. When he landed inside this cave, it was the same as you were going into the biggest dining hall you ever saw in your life. This place was huge, just like a monster house. And it was all hung with all the fishing things under the sun, stuff that was salvaged from boats that went down. There were barrels and boxes and nets and creels and everything under the sun that was needed for fishing. And sitting on a stool in the middle of the floor beside this big fire was the biggest old man that Jack had ever seen in his life. And his hair was down his back and it was fiery red, so was his beard. And he was stone blind. When he spoke his voice rumbled right through the cave inside.

'What can I do for ye, boy?' he said. 'Come forward, boy, where I can hear ye closer. And what do ye want of me?'

'Well,' Jack said, 'I've come a long way. You're Blind Rory, known as Blind Rory.'

He said, 'I am Blind Rory.'

He said, 'I want to buy a net.'

'What do you want a net for, boy?' he said. 'To catch fish?'

'No,' says Jack, 'I don't want a net to catch fish. I want a net to catch a mermaid.'

'What?' says Blind Rory, and his voice sure it echoed right through the cave. 'Boy, do you mean to tell me,' he said, 'that you've come all this distance – and ought to have more sense, a young man o' your age who would want to catch a mermaid. The best hing you can do, son, is go straight back the way you cam and forget that you ever saw a mermaid!'

Jack said, 'Look, I've got money, and I want to buy a net fae you! And you're the only person in the country that can give me a net.'

The old man said, *'Look what I'm tellin ye, if I give ye a net, whatever you get in it is yours.*

'Well,' says Jack, 'that's what I want.'

'But,' he says, 'what if ye get in it is *no* what ye want . . . ye'll have to keep!'

'Well,' says Jack, 'that'll be up to me.'

'Well,' says the old man, 'if ye're persistent and you want a net, I'll give ye a net. But remember, what ye catch in it will be yours and yours only! And I canna gie ye nae help after that. But I'll give ye a net, I'll no charge ye for it, laddie. Ye've come too far. But ye willna tak nae advice fae me, and you've been well warned by your mother,' as Jack tellt him about his mother and his auntie, 'and,' he said, 'the old men of the village. And you will no listen. But I'm tellin ye again, the best thing you can do is forget about me, net and mermaid and go straight back as if nothing had happened to ye!'

'No,' says Jack, 'I want ye to give me a net to catch a mermaid.'

'Well,' says the old man, 'ye're really determined. Go
over there to that wall.' And over Jack goes. He says, 'Shove
your hand in that big canvas bag.' Jack shoved his hand in
the big canvas bag. And he pulled out this net, like a poke
with corks on it round the top, like a long bag. 'That,' says
the old man, 'is the net you want, And I'm givin it to you
free. You're the first man that ever cam into this cave
since ever I took over here, and I hope you'll be the last.
But remember, the minute you take this net out o' this place
you canna come back, or I canna give you no help. Whatever ye catch in it is yer own, or whatever ye get you must
keep!'

'Well,' says Jack, 'that's what I want.'

'Well,' says the old man, 'we'll say no more about it.' He
says to the lassie, 'Give him somethin to eat.'

The lassie gave him a good feed. They sat down. And he
never mentioned it no more to the old man, and they cracked
a long long while. Jack bade the old man and his grand-
daughter 'good-bye', took his net in his pack and set sail for
home. He travelled and he travelled, on and on and on and
on, travelled all the way back the way he came till he landed
back in his mother's house. And his mother was surprised to
see him.

'Well, laddie,' she said, 'ye've been away a long long
while.'

'Aye, Mother,' he said, 'but it was worth-while.'

'Maybe,' says the old woman, 'maybe it was worth-while,
maybe it wasna. Did ye see Blind Rory?'

'Aye, Mother,' he says, 'I saw a lot o' folk. And they all
gien me the same advice. What is it about the mermaid that
youse folk dinna like?'

She said, 'Jack, ye're too young to understand.'

He says, 'I'm no young, I'm twenty years of age. And I'm
bound to ken what I want – I want the mermaid!'

41

'Right,' says his mother, 'you go ahead and you catch your mermaid, but remember, ye paid nae heed tae naebody. So whatever happens to ye when ye get a mermaid and what ye do wi it is up to yersel!'

'Well,' says Jack, 'can folk no let it be that way? And let me do what I want!'

So his old mother gives him his supper and he goes to his bed, and he takes the net with him in case his mother would destroy it! Up to his bed with him, puts the net below his head. All night he couldna sleep, he couldna wait till daylight till he got back to the beach. Now this place where Jack's supposed to see the mermaid was a long narrow lagoon where the water came in, it was awful awful deep. And there was a narrow channel in between. And every time he seen her playing in this wee round pool, when he ran down to get close to her she escaped through the channel. And he made up his mind that he was going to get a net that he could set in the channel, so that when she went back out – she wouldna see it coming in – but he would catch her on the road back out.

Right, so the next day was a lovely sunny day and away he goes. He sets his net, and he sits and he sits and he sits, he sits and sits till it gets kind o' gloamin dark, and a mist comes down. He hears splishing and splashing in the water. He says, 'That's her!' Then he pulls the string and his net opens up. And he runs down . . . sheook – in she goes to the bag. He catches the bag and he sees the long hair, and the fish's tail and the hands, the face. He pulls the net tight and he flings it on his back. Then he makes back to his mother's house with it hard as he could.

But by sheer good luck who was up at his mother's house at the same time seeing his mother, because she wasna keeping very well, but his old auntie. In comes Jack to the house, 'Mother, Mother,' he says, 'light the lamps!'

'What for, laddie?'

He says, 'I got a mermaid!'

The old woman was surprised. 'Mermaid, laddie,' she says, 'there's nae such a thing as a mermaid. I tellt ye that . . .'

'But Mother,' he says, 'listen! I got the mermaid and I've got her in the net, I got her in my net. Blind Rory's net did the trick – I got my mermaid!'

'All right,' says his mother, 'I'll light the lamps.'

So his old auntie rose and she lighted the two paraffin lamps. And Jack dropped the net on the floor and shaked it out. He looked. Sister dear, you want to see what he shaked out – an old woman about seventy years of age! And every tooth the length of my finger, and her two eyes staring in her head and her hair straggly, and this fish's tail on her and her hands with big long nails and them curled. And she's looking at Jack and she's spitting at him. But she could speak as good as they.

'Aye,' she said, 'laddie, you catcht me. You catcht me and I'm yours and you'll keep me.'

Now the old auntie who had come in about she looked. The old auntie gave one roar, and she said, 'Laddie, laddie, laddie, Jack, Jack, do ye ken what ye've gotten? You wouldna listen to naebody.'

'Aye,' he said, 'I ken what I've gotten, I've got a mermaid.'

She says, 'Laddie, that's nae mermaid. You've got yourself a sea witch!'

'What,' he says, 'auntie?'

She said, 'You've got yourself a sea witch.'

'Aye,' says the old witch, 'you've got me! You've catcht me in Blind Rory's net, and I'm yours. And you'll look after me. I'll do everything in my power to mak you suffer for what you've done to me.'

'I'll take ye back to the sea,' says Jack, 'and fling ye in.'

'Na, na,' says the sea witch, 'that'll no do nae good!' She spits on the two old women, Jack's mother and his auntie, and her eyes are blazing at them. The old women were that feart o' her they wouldna come near her. So she commanded Jack to do everything for her, give her something to eat, make her a bed and do everything. 'Now,' she said to Jack, 'Jack, every day you'll carry me to the shore and you'll carry me back, and you'll let me bathe and you'll wait for me. Ye'll tend me hand and foot for the rest o' yer days! That's yer punishment when ye wouldna listen – ye had no right settin a net and catchin me. I am a sea witch. You shall be punished for the rest o' your days.'

Jack was in an awful state. He was sorry then, he said, 'I wish I would hae listened to my old auntie and listened to the old men and listened to Blind Rory.' But there was nothing he could do about it now. He said, 'I'll fling her back in the sea, Mother.'

'You mightna fling me back in the sea,' says the old witch, 'because I'll just be back here the next minute. And I'll go on punishin you for the rest o' your days.'

'Well,' said Jack, 'so it may be, we'll see.'

'We'll see!' said the sea witch.

So Jack never got a minute's peace, day out and day in she made him do everything for her. She wanted the best of fish, she wanted the best of meat, she wanted carried and a bed made for her, she wanted everything done for her, she wanted carried to the sea and carried back from the sea twice a day. And the farther Jack was carrying her the heavier she was getting. Till Jack got that weak he could hardly move with her, and he didna ken what to do. He was in an awful state. The old auntie had banned herself from coming near the house. And the old women hid themselves, they wouldna come near the sea witch. Jack's mother tellt him, 'As long as it's in this house I'm no comin back to the house. I'm goin off wi my old sister.' The two old women cleared out and left Jack with the witch. And he was in the house by himself.

But yin day he managed to get away by himself, and he cut along the shore. The sea witch was sleeping, and he made for his old auntie's house. He was out of breath from running because he didna want to be long away. He landed in and his old auntie was sitting.

'Oh, it's you, Jack,' she says, 'what happened to you now? Where is she?'

'I think she's sleeping,' he said, 'till the sun goes down. Then I have to take her back to the sea. Auntie, ye'll have to help me! I'm sair wrought, I dinna ken what to do wi her. She's got me punished to death. When she shouts on me I carry her down the stair, because she canna move without a wet tail. When her tail gets dry I have to carry her down and back to the sea, keep her tail wet.'

'Well,' says the auntie, 'you wouldna listen to me, would you? Nor you wouldna listen to Rory. But now you've proved your point. And you were well warned. But if ye ever get free o' this woman, this is bound to be a lesson to ye. But I'll tell ye, now listen to me and do what I tell ye tonight when ye get a chance. You'll go back up, Jack, and you'll tak her down when she wants down to the kitchen. Put her beside the fire for to gie her her supper. Once her back's turned to ye, ye'll snap off her hair wi yer mother's big shears. And ye'll mak a rope out o' her hair. Tie it round her middle and tie her hands and tie up her tail wi it – from her ain hair – and fling her into the sea, let her go to the bottom!'

'Right,' says Jack, 'I'll do that.' Back he goes.

But he was nae sooner coming in the door when he hears this roar, 'Are ye there, are ye there, are ye there?' This was the sea witch roaring, 'Come at once and carry me down!'

Jack ran . . . but before he went up the stairs he searched his mother's house, in the kitchen, and he got his mother's big pair of shears. He put them on the mantelpiece. Up the stairs he went and he carried this thing down with the long hair and the big long teeth, this sea witch. He put her sitting alongside the fire.

She says, 'Get me something to eat, the best o' fish, Jack!' Oh, she wanted everything under the sun, it had to be everything o' the best.

But she was sitting eating. She could eat, ye ken, her two hands were like any human being's, only for her tail. Jack got round her back and he took the shears. He catcht all her hair – oh, long hair, it was hanging on the floor – and he snip, snip, snip, snipped the whole lot off. And she screamed at him and swung round. If she had had feet instead of a tail she would have torn him to ribbons. But Jack kept out of her reach. And she flapped and flapped and flapped and screamed and carried on right round the floor, roaring and screaming the worst way she could what she was going to do on him. But Jack kept catching this hair. And he twisted it into a rope, and jumped on top o' her, and he catcht her. With the long hair he tied her two hands at her back, he wapped all this round her. And he put her across his shoulder. She's screaming murder! And he carried her on his back back to the lagoon. He flung her in! And down she went. And he stood. The bubbles came up, bubbles came up.

He must have stood for ten minutes and then he says, 'That's the end o' her. That's her finished.' He was just going to turn and walk away when he sees the bubbles coming back up again. And up from the water comes this head, and looks at him. Jack looks and he sees the bonniest mermaid that ever he's seen in his life, the original yin that he saw the first time.

And she sat just within reach o' him. She came out, her head out of the water and she spoke to him. 'Well, Jack,' she said, 'for a long while you've tried to catch me. And ye ken what you've catcht. You've catcht a sea witch. That's the end o' her. But ye'll never catch me because I'll no be nae use to ye. The best thing ye can do is forget all about me, and never again – let that be a lesson to you – never never try and catch a mermaid!' And she disappeared.

And Jack turned round. He walked home and tellt this story to his mother. From that day on, till the day that he went off the earth Jack never again tried to catch a mermaid. And that's the last o' my story.

THE DEVIL'S SALT MILL

Old Magog the Devil's mother was a wee bit upset because the Devil himself, her son, was wandering round the furnace of Hell picking up this thing, picking up that thing and looking at his mother. She could see that something was troubling him. And this upset old Magog because she loved her son dearly. She said, 'Laddie, what's wrong wi ye? Man, ye never gie me nae peace, ye never stop for a minute. Ye're pickin up things an flingin things down, pokin the fire and doin all these things round the furnace. What's botherin ye?'

So the Devil turns round and he looks at his mother, he says, 'Mother, I'm miserable.'

She says, 'What are you miserable for, son?'

He says, 'It's weeks and weeks and weeks since I've had a soul to torment. I'm fed up tormenting the same old souls. It's nae pleasure for me. If I only had new souls, people I've never met before to torment it would make me happy.'

So his old mother thought and thought to herself, she would like to help her son. She knew that out on earth there were hundreds of souls. People were not dying as fast as they should have been. And this made the Devil unhappy. So she looked all around the caverns of Hell, there was the great fire burning and there were the cages o' all the imps sitting looking out with their ugly nails and their ugly faces. They were trapped in Hell to torment the souls who came there

49

from earth. She said, 'I would like to help my laddie, he's unhappy. If I dinna help him, he'll gang awa for weeks and months an' no be back. And when he's gone I'm sad.'

Then she looked up on a stone shelf beside the cavern of the fireplace of Hell, and there sat a little mill. Now this was a favourite possession of the Devil. Where he had gotten it his mother did not know. It was a salt mill. When the Devil was lonely and sad sometimes he would take the little salt mill on his knee, he would caress it, and put it back on the shelf. And his mother knew that he loved this mill. But where it came from she never knew. But then she knew if she wanted to make her son happy she would have to get him some souls to torment, people who would come to Hell for the trouble they had caused on earth.

So then she walks up with her shawl over her shoulders and she looks all around. The Devil was busy poking the fire and turning the coals on the fire. And she snaps the little salt mill! She puts it under her old black shawl, which was thousands of years old. Then she says, 'If he's needing something, I'll have to help him.' And then old Magog was gone from Hell.

She travelled up the far journey from the pits of Hell till she came to earth. She had a view in her mind that if she could give this salt mill to someone who would appreciate it, then she could help the Devil. So she landed in a small village and the first place she came to was a junk shop. But this junk shop was owned by a rich merchant who had travelled far across the land buying all the queer things that he could see, bringing them back and selling them to the people for a large profit. He travelled to India, he travelled all through the East with his ships at sea. He was rich, he was miserable, he was mean. But he had ships at sea. So into the shop walked the old woman with her black shawl over her head. And she took the little wooden mill and she put it on the table.

50

THE DEVIL'S SALT MILL

The merchant stood in behind the table and he looked, and he spied this little salt mill. It was made of wood with a little wheel on the top and a little handle that you turned slowly. You put rock salt on the top and you turned it, it grinded the salt to make it ready for eating.

So the old woman said to the rich merchant, 'Mister! Mister, I have something to sell.'

'Oh come, come, old woman,' he said, 'ay, come old woman!' He rubbed his hands, 'I am always interested in something to sell. What have you got?'

She said, 'I have a little salt mill.'

'Oh,' said the merchant, 'a salt mill! I have seen a few of these in my time but I've never saw one actually like this one. What do you want for it?'

She says, 'Nothing. It belongs to my son, and I want to give it to you as a present.'

'But,' he says, 'my dear, it's hard to get rock salt nowadays. You know this is very old, this mill is very old. There's no many has rock salt anymore.'

'Oh but,' she says, 'mister, ye dinna need any rock salt. All ye have do do is just *ask it* to give you salt, and you'll get as much as you want.'

'Aye,' the old merchant said, he didna believe this. But he thought the old woman was kind of crazy. 'But,' he said, 'what would you like for it?'

She said, 'I dinna want nothing for it, merchant. I just want to give it to ye, because somebody maybe'll use it, or you could use it! But just if ye need salt – just ask it! It'll give ye salt.'

The merchant didna believe this, but he said, 'Okay, I'll take it, old woman.' And he took it, he put in on the shelf. And he looked round, the old woman was gone. She'd vanished as if she had never existed. But the merchant looked at it for a long time, it was a beautiful little salt mill, like he had never seen before in his life. And he really liked it.

But anyway a few days came to pass. It was time for the merchant once again to go with his boat on a journey to the northern seas to sell his wares, and he took everything from his shop that he would trade, bales of this and stuff of that. And he had thirty-three seamen on his ship, it was 33 plus himself. And they were going on a long journey off into the East. Because this is what the merchant did all his life, collected all these things, bought all his stuff, took a boat and loaded it and sailed into many different ports selling all these things he had collected.

So after the boat was loaded he said to the captain, 'Is everything loaded, everything out of the shop?' Everything he needed to take with him . . . and then the merchant looked round, he saw the wee salt mill. He said, 'Maybe I'll need you.' And he picked the salt mill up and he took it with him. He took it to his own private cabin and put it in there.

Back in Hell old Magog she smiled to herself and rubbed her hands in glee, because she could see that the merchant had took the salt mill with him.

So it came morning and it was time to sail. A great sailing ship, ten-master, sailed off from the port with the merchant and 33 sailors. They took off into the East. Then after some hours at sea the merchant came down for lunch and he was sitting down to eat. He said to the cook, 'Where is the salt?'

'Oh, master,' he said, 'We've took many things, but that's one thing – we have never tooken any salt – one thing we forgot.'

Back in Hell the Devil was sitting with his old mother, he was still stirring the fire. And then he looked around and he saw that his mill was gone. 'Mother,' the Devil said, 'have you tooken my salt mill?' This was his prize possession which he always took every night and caressed on his knee, because he loved it.

'Aye son,' she said, 'it was me.'

'But Mother,' he said, 'why did ye take my salt mill? It sat there for hundreds of years. And it's mine!'

'Son, you're unhappy.'

'But,' he said, 'ye're making me more unhappy. Ye took my salt mill, didn't ye? What did ye do with it, where did you put it?'

She says, 'I gave it away.'

He says, 'You gave my salt mill away, Mother?'

She says, 'Yes, I gave your salt mill away. I gave it to a merchant.'

He said, 'Mother, ye gave my salt mill to a merchant? The only prize possession I had in my life which I loved, which you do not understand nothing about! Mother, I'm going to punish you! I'm goin to treat you like you've never been treated before in your life!'

She says, 'Son, just wait a couple o' days. I'll take any punishment you can give me. But just give me a couple o' days.'

'Mother,' he says, Mother, I'm goin to punish you like I've never punished any soul in their lifetime, Mother. I'll put you in the fire, I'll roast you, Mother, I'll do anything with ye, I'll make you drink boilin lead, unless you get my salt mill.'

She said, 'Son, your salt mill is on its way across the sea.'

'Mother,' he said, 'what do ye think ye're doing on me?'

She says, 'Wait an see.'

But the old Magog and her son the Devil argued and argued back and forward. Until the Devil said, 'Mother, I'll give ye two days . . .'

And the old Magog she sat back and she smiled to herself.

But meantime out in the sea went the merchant with his 33 sailors and himself. It was lunchtime. And the merchant was sitting down to have a meal but there was no salt. He called to the cook again, 'Can we have some salt for wir dinner?'

53

'Oh master,' said the cook, 'I beg your forgiveness. We forgot to take salt, we've not a drop of salt on the boat.'

Merchant said, 'Well, we can't eat without salt.' And then he said, 'Wait a minute, I have something I got from an old woman. And she told me all I need to do is ask for salt, and we'll have salt.' So he walked into his cabin and he took his beautiful little wooden mill with the wheel at the back. He placed it on the table in front of all the sailors and the cook and everybody else. He said, 'This old woman told me all we have to do is "ask for salt".'

Everyone looked around, they said, 'How can you get salt from the like o' that?'

And the merchant said, 'Can we have some salt?'

Then the little wheel began to turn. Non-stop the salt came and it came and it came and it came. It came and it came and it filled the table, it filled the floor. It filled the whole hold, it filled the cabins, it filled everything. Non-stop went the mill till the merchant was buried and the sailors were buried to their waists in salt. And they cried, 'Stop, stop, stop!' But there was no way could they stop the mill. On and on went the mill producing salt after salt after salt till soon everything in the ship was full, the hold was full, the cabins was full, the wheelhouse, everything was full in the ship, everything! One day had passed.

In Hell the Devil said, 'Mother, you have another day to return my salt mill.'

She rubbed her hands in glee did old Magog. She said, 'Give me another day!'

And then the mill went on producing the salt, till the ship could take not another grain. And naturally down went the ship in the sea, sailors 33, merchant, salt mill sank to the bottom of the sea.

Then back in Hell the Devil had a great surprise. Because into Hell came 33 sailors and a merchant! And the Devil looked around, he said, 'Mother, we have visitors!'

She said, 'Yes, son, ye have visitors. Ye have sailors. Ye have a merchant who is evil. And I am sure they will keep ye happy for a few days.'

And the Devil said, 'Mother, what's about my salt mill?'

'Well,' she said, 'Son, I gave the salt mill to a merchant who took it aboard his ship, who demanded for salt – and your mill sank his ship to the bottom of the sea. And there you got yourself 33 souls plus the merchant. Won't that keep you happy for some time?'

'But,' he said, 'Mother, what about my salt mill?'

She said, 'Son, it is in the bottom of the sea and there it remains. Turning till this day.'

And the Devil smiled at his old mother, 'Well,' he said, 'Mother, I'll forget about the salt mill for the time bein. I still think about it, but 33 souls and a merchant will keep me happy for some time to come.'

Meanwhile the salt mill still lies in the bottom of the sea still turning. And that's why the sea is so salty, and that's why till this day it's called the Devil's Paddling Pool!

THE WOODCUTTER AND THE DEVIL

A long time ago an old woodcutter lived in the forest and he
cut timber for a living. He took it with a little handcart to the
village to sell it to the local community. His wife had died and
left him with three little boys, and he loved these children
from his heart. But oh, he missed his wife terribly. Every
evening when he'd put the children to bed, he would sit there
lonely by the fireside and put some logs on, say to himself, 'I
wish she was here to direct me and tell me what's to happen in
the morning. Well,' he said, 'there's nothing else for it, I must
rear the boys up the best way I can.' Before they were school
age the poor woodcutter took them with him to the forest and
showed them how to work in the wood. They helped him
lifting axes and doing things around the forest. Then at night-
time he took them by his feet by the fireside and told them
stories, many stories.

So one day the oldest of the boys turned round and said,
'Daddy, I love your stories. But can you not tell us about
something else? There are many other wonderful things,
Daddy, to tell us than stories about trees and wind and
windblown trees.'

'Son, I would love to tell you other stories, but,' he said,
'me telling you about something else would make you far too
inquisitive, to want to understand about things out in the
world which you're not fit for!'

57

'But,' he said, 'Daddy, we don't want to stay here and be woodcutters. We don't want to grow up like you, to be an old man spending your life in the forest cutting trees and getting no richer or no better off.'

'Well,' he said, 'I've tried my best, boys. I've brought you up and worked hard for you.'

'But Daddy,' he said, 'this is not a life for us – we want to be someone special! Daddy, tell us what to do!'

'Well,' he said, 'I'll tell you, you stay home today, tidy up the house and feed your little brothers. And when I come back tonight I'll tell you what to do.'

So he went into the forest and cut trees as usual. And he sat down there by himself. 'Isn't it terrible,' he said, 'my wife is gone, gone forever. And I'm left with three little boys, they're getting so grown up I don't know what to do with them. I'll never make enough money to give them an education or anything. They're so inquisitive and they want to understand so many things . . . *God Almighty, could you help me!*'

But no thought came to his mind.

He said, '*Jesus Christ, could you help me!*'

But no thought came to his mind.

He said, '*Would the Devil o' Hell help me? I would give my soul to the Devil this night if I had money to give my boys a good education!*

And then there was a rumble o' thunder, it got dark.

He said, 'I'd better get up and make my way back.'

But lo and behold there before him stood this tall dark man dressed in a long cape, 'I heard you old man,' he said, 'I heard you!'

'Well,' he said, 'I was speaking out aloud, I was cursing to myself.'

'Oh, of course,' he said, 'you were cursing. But you mentioned my name.'

He said, 'Did I? And who are you?'

He said, 'I am the Devil!'

'The Devil!' he said. 'At last *someone* has come to help me!'

'Of course,' said the Devil, 'I've come to help you. Your god wouldn't help you, your Jesus wouldn't help you, would he? But I'm the Devil and I've come to help you. What is it you want?'

'Well,' said the old woodcutter, 'you know what I want. There's me, my wife's dead and gone to Hell or Heaven, I don't know.'

'Well,' the Devil said, 'I never saw her.'

'Well,' the old man said, 'she must be in a better place. Look, I've three grown up boys and they're getting kind of inquisitive. They want a better life, they don't want to spend their lives with me – their father in the forest. How can I give them a better life, I'm only a poor woodcutter making a few shillings to get food for them?'

The Devil says, 'I can help you.'

'Oh,' he says, 'I wish you would help me . . . Devil o' Hell, would you help me!'

He says, 'I'll help you. What do you need?'

He says, 'Money! I need money! I want to put them off to school, to college. I want to make men of them, so's they'll grown up and be great men.'

Devil says, 'No problem. I'll give you all the money you want. But what have I to get in return?'

'Oh Devil,' he says, 'you can get anything you want of me. You can have *me!*'

Devil says, 'Is that true? Can I have *you? Can* I have you, heart and soul and body?'

'Devil,' he said, 'you give me money and you can have anything you want!'

Devil says, 'Go back home tonight, go to your kist in your bedroom – it will be full! But I'll be back for you in ten years time.'

'Done!' says the old woodcutter. 'No problem, you can have me, heart and soul. By that time my boys'll be grown up and be young men, they'll not need me anymore.'

True enough, he wanders home a happy old woodcutter. When he lands home the boys have a few vegetables and a little meat on the table. They'd cleaned the house up, you know. And he had a little bite to eat. He walked in to an old kist that he had in his own room, and he lifted the lid . . . it was full of old clothes and things. He pulled the old clothes apart and there in the bottom it was packed with gold sovereigns.

He said, 'The Devil has told the truth. Now I have the money! So naturally he called his three boys together and he said, 'Boys, listen. Last night we had a discussion and you wanted to be great men. So I'm going to pay for you, I'm going to send you off to school! What would you like to be?'

So the oldest one said, 'Well, Father, I would like to be a minister. Because I know, Father, you lost my mother . . . and I want to preach the word of God to all the people.'

'Is that what you want to be?' says the father.

'Yes, Father.'

'Well, a minister you can be.' So he called the second son before him and said, 'What would you like to be my son?'

He said, 'I would like to be a doctor.'

'Oh,' he said, 'no problem, son, I'll put you to college, I have plenty of money to put you to college now!'

'But, Father,' he said, 'how have you become so rich?'

He says, 'Son, don't you worry about it.' And to the youngest one he said, 'What would you like to be my little son?'

He said, 'Father, I've talked to you and you've given me some very interesting discussions, and I would like to be a lawyer.'

'Well,' he said, 'son, no problem! You shall be a lawyer.'

So the next day the father, the old woodcutter, made arrangements to send his three young sons off to college wherever they wanted to go. He sent them off, paid all their expenses, lived by himself and they grew up. And one became a great minister. And one became a great doctor. And one became a great lawyer. Nine years had passed. Now the boys were grown up. And one evening there was a knock at the door.

The oldest son came in, he said, 'Father, I have come to visit you.'

'Oh,' he said, 'my son, I am pleased that you have come to visit me. Because you know I haven't got long to go.'

'Why not, Father?' he said.

'Well,' he said, 'it's a long story. Because you see, son, I sold my soul to the Devil just for the sake of you. And he'll be coming for me tonight.'

'Oh dear, Father,' he said, 'we don't want to lose you – you're our father and you've done so much for us. Do my brothers know about this?'

'No,' he said, 'your brothers don't know about this.'

He said, 'When is he coming?'

'Well,' he says, 'tonight at twelve o'clock.'

He says, 'Father, can I wait?'

'Oh,' he says, 'I don't want you to meet the Devil, son – you're a minister! You could never meet the Devil. He's coming!'

'Father,' he says, 'can I wait?'

But they sat and they talked till twelve o'clock. And lo and behold there was the rattle of thunder and a rattle at the door – and in walks the Devil!

He said, 'Okay, old man, get up! I have come for you.'

And the minister got up. He had his crucifix hanging by his neck. 'Just a moment,' he said, 'you know this is my father!'

'I know,' said the Devil, and he held his hand before his eyes. 'I know,' he said, 'I know, I've come for your father.'

'Well, look,' says the minister, 'you know I preach the word of God.'

'Don't mention that word to me,' says the Devil, 'I don't want to hear it!'

'Well, look,' he says, 'I have never seen my father for many years. For my sake . . .'

'Not for your sake,' said the Devil, 'in any way – I've come for your father.'

'But I have never had time to spend with my father. Could you give him another year just to please me?'

The Devil said, 'Right, look . . . if you take that thing from your neck so that I can talk to you, I'll think about it.'

So the minister turned his crucifix to the back of his neck.

'Now,' he says, 'we can look at you. I'll tell you, I'll give your father one more year just because you've been away for a while. But then I'm coming for him!'

'Okay,' said the minister, 'I'll make my peace with my father before that time.'

And then the Devil was gone.

So the minister and his son they had a nice time together, and he went back to his parish. And he stayed in the parish, left his father alone.

But a year had nearly passed. Then came the next son, the doctor, to visit his father. They had sat there talking and discussing things when lo and behold there was another rumble of thunder. And the door opened – in walks the Devil again!

Doctor said, 'Who is this, Father?'

'Oh, it's an old friend of mine,' he said, 'son. He has come to see me. You know I have a long story to tell you, but I can't tell you right now.'

'But,' he said, 'who is it, Father?'

He said, 'It's the Devil.'

'The Devil?' said the doctor.

'Of course,' he said, 'the Devil, son. Look, all thon money I put you through college with didn't belong to me. It belonged to the Devil! And I've sold my soul to him and he's come for me. He's taking me tonight.'

'Oh,' the doctor said, 'so he's taking you tonight. Well, we'll have to see about this, Father.'

The Devil spoke, 'Old man,' he said, 'the time has come. I've given you one chance and no more.'

So the doctor son stood up, he said, 'Look, Devil, I know who you are! You're the Devil.'

'Of course I'm the Devil,' he said, 'I've come for your father!'

'But you can't take my father,' he said.

'But,' he said, 'your father has sold his soul to me. I gave him my money – how do you think you got to college to be a doctor? How do you think you've saved so many souls . . . I'm angry about you! You have saved people that I could have had!'

'Well,' the doctor said, 'that's my business. I've been working hard.'

'You're a nice senisble young man, you've been working hard, that's true,' said the Devil.

'But anyway,' he said, 'look . . . could you give my father one more year? My youngest brother of all comes back next year, he is just about to become a lawyer. And if you took him away now, my youngest brother would be upset. Please, Devil, would you give my father one more year?'

'Okay,' said the Devil, 'one more year – no more!' Like that the Devil was gone.

So then the woodcutter and his son spent a lovely night together, and he had to go back to his practice, you know. So another year passed by. The old man was quite happy by himself. And then there was a knock at the door and in came the youngest son.

He says, 'Father, at last! That's it, I am a lawyer now, Father!'

And his father was so happy to see him. He threw his arms round him and cuddled him, he said, 'My baby, my youngest son! You've really made it.'

'Yes, Father,' he said, 'I have. Let's go in and have a dine together and have a drink together.'

But he said, 'Son, do you know what the time is . . . tonight I can't spend much time with you.'

'Why, Father,' he said, 'I've come all the way to see you? Aren't you happy to see me?'

'Of course, my son,' he said. 'I've had your brothers here, they've gone after their visits. Now you have come, but I can't spend much time with you.'

'Why, Father,' he said, 'Why can't you spend time with me?'

'Well,' he said, 'son, it's a long story. You know all that money I put you through college with – it was not mine. It belonged to the Devil.'

'The Devil?' said the lawyer.

'Of course, son,' he said, 'I sold my soul to the Devil to get you through college. And tonight he's coming for me.'

'Father,' he said, 'Father, I've not time to spend with you?'

'Well, son,' he said, 'this is the last chance! Your brother had a chance and your second brother had a chance, and now it's your turn.'

'But Father,' he said, 'I just can't let you go away with the Devil – I've only come here!'

They sat and talked, and then there was the rattle of thunder again! And the door opened – in walks the Devil.

Rubbed his hands together, he said, 'Okay, old man, no more chances. Who's this you have here with you?'

He said, 'This is my son.'

He said, 'A son?'

'Yes,' he said, 'this is the son who has just come through college, he's a lawyer.'

'Oh, he's a lawyer?' says the Devil. 'Well, they tell me lawyers are very clever.'

'Well,' says the woodcutter, 'he's a clever young man, lawyers are very clever.'

So the lawyer turned, he said, 'I heard the story, Devil, and about the extensions you gave my other brothers. Look, I've only come back for a wee while to see my father. We haven't much time . . . you can't take him away from me!'

'Well,' the Devil said, 'I gave your two brothers one chance each. And it wouldn't be fair for me – even the Devil – to not give you a little chance. How long would you like your father to stay with you?'

'Oh,' said the lawyer, and he walked over to the table. Burning on the table was a candle and it was burnt nearly to the bottom. He said, 'Look, Devil, I know you've been kind. You've been more generous than anyone, even more generous than God. You gave my brother a year and you gave my other brother a year. And all I'm asking you, Devil,' he says, 'can I spend a little time with my father – until that wee bit of candle burns to the end of the wick?'

'Oh,' the Devil said, 'Certainly, no problem, no problem. That's not too bad, you can have your wish.'

And the lawyer walks up and he blows out the wee candle. He puts it in his pocket.

And the Devil is furious! He says, 'A minister could not beat the Devil and neither could a doctor. He said, *It only takes a lawyer!*'

JACK AND THE DEVIL'S GOLD

Jack was reared with his old mother, they lived in this cottage and everything she done was just for the sake o' getting him reared up the best she could. But one morning she says to him, 'Jack, ye'll have to gang to the town and get two-three bits o' messages today again.'

'I dinna mind goin for the messages, Mother, but look,' he says, 'can ye gie me a shilling to mysel?'

She says, 'What are ye wantin a shilling for?'

'Ye ken what I want a shilling for,' he says, 'for to get a wee, wee bit "thing" to mysel.'

'Look, bad luck's goin to follow you yet,' she said, 'ower the heids o' this drink, this carry-on. Drinkin is goin to get you into serious trouble.'

He says, 'Mother, for all the drink that I get it'll no do me much harm.' But anyway, he hemmed and hawed and he managed to beg her for half a crown to go to the town.

'Now,' she says, 'remember, I ken that you're goin to come back the short cut through the wood. And Jack, if it's late, dinna come back through there, I tellt ye an awfa bing o' times. 'Cause I'll tell ye somethin, some o' these times the Devil'll get ye comin back through the short cut!'

Now where Jack stayed in this wee house with his mother, if he went round the road it was about two miles to the wee village. But if he came back through the wood by the short

67

cut, he had to pass this big clift in this rock, and it was a dreary path through the wood. But away Jack went to the town and he bought his two-three bits o' messages for his mother, whatever he needed. And in, to the pub, he spent his half crown. And he got hisself a good goin drink. By the time he got out o' the pub it was about ten o'clock. He got his mother's wee bit messages on his back, and he went back the road.

But when he came to the crossroads he said, 'Man, it's a long bit round about that road. The're naethin's goin to bother me goin through this short cut.' His mother warned him not to take it at night. He went it two-three times during the day, he kent it, knew the road well. But he'd never come through it at night before. It was ten o'clock, the month of October and the moon was shining clearly. And with the drink in his head he said, 'Ach I canna walk that bit the night, I'm going back through the short cut.'

So back he comes. And he travels on, he travels on. But before getting near the house he had to come to a bad bend in the road, and there was a face o' a clift. Then there was a path that led ye down to the house. And the moon was shining clear. Jack's walking on the wee pad and he's dottering on, ye ken a wee drink on him! And he looks – lyin right on the pad shinin – a gold sovereign.

Jack bends and he picks it up, brother, and he looks. 'Oh dear-dear,' he says, 'if I'd hae come this way the first time I could hae haen that, I could hae haen that drunk. But it'll keep to the mornin.' But he'd only tooken another two steps . . . another yin! And after he'd tooken another step – another one!

But these coins weared away up the pad. And he followed them, he picked them up as he went. He came to the face o' the clift. He looked, there was a dark hole and he could see light, a light . . . and he seen a fire shinin in a monster cave in

68

the face o' the clift! He says, 'I never kent this place was here before. Maybe it's an old buck gadgie* with a fire. Maybe he's lost his money, maybe he stole it fae somebody. He dropped it from a hole in the bag or something, he's in there wi all that loor!† Tsst, I'm goin in for a crack to him, maybe he's got somethin to drink!' He walks in, into the face o' the clift. He sees this big fire and here this man's sittin.

Tall dark man sittin at the fire, 'Come on, Jack!' he said. 'I've been waitin for you for a long long while, Jack, come on in!'

So Jack walked further in. But a funny thing about the fire was, the sticks was burning but they werena seemin to be deein out. Shadows was round the wall, Jack could see the shadows of the fire was making droll faces on the front of the wall.

He says, 'Sit down, Jack.' Jack sat down. He says, 'Ye never done what yer mother tellt ye, did ye?'

'No,' says Jack, 'I never done what my mother tellt me.'

He said, 'Yer mother tellt ye not to come back the short cut tonight, didn't she?'

'Aye,' said Jack. 'But if I hadna come back I wouldna hae found the money.'

He said, 'What money did ye find, Jack?'

He said, 'I found money on the road up. And it led me into this cave. You stole it and you lost it. It's mine now! You stole it fae somebody.'

He said, 'How much did you get?'

Jack said, 'I got a good few onyway.' Hand in his pocket, brother, nothing! Not a haet! He emptied his pocket outside in – nothin!

And this man laughed. 'Na, na, Jack,' he said, 'ye mightna look in yer pocket, laddie, the're nothin in yer pocket. Ye like money, Jack, don't ye?'

* buck gadgie – tramp man
† loor – money

69

'Aye', said Jack, 'I like money. I was reared with my mother since my father dee'd. I dinna remember much about him. And me and her got a hard time o' it.'

And he said, 'Ye like a drink, Jack?'

'O-oh,' he said, 'I like a drink all right, I love a drink.'

And he said, 'You spend every wee copper that yer mother's got for the sake o' buyin drink! And she's to do wantin a lot o' things that she could buy for the money you spend.'

Jack said, 'That's got nothin to do wi you.'

He said, 'Jack, that's got an awfa lot to do wi me! Look, if you want money, the're a boxfull there, help yersel, tak as much as ye want!'

Now, when Jack sat with his mother at the fire in their house, it was a peat fire they had. And Jack used to be fond o' sittin at the fire with his bare feet. And they always used to keep a creel o' peats at the fireside. When the fire burnt down, Jack was lyin back gettin a good heat, his mother used to tell Jack to put a bit peat on the fire. And he could bend down, he could lift a peat with his toe and put it on the fire with his foot, his bare foot – to save him from gettin up. Touch o' laziness, ye see! And Jack had practised this for years and he'd got that good at it, well, Jack was as clever with his foot as he was with his hand . . .

So, the Devil said, 'There's plenty in the box, Jack, help yerself!' So Jack put his hand in the box, lifted it up, a handful. Then, two hands, when he got it in his two hands . . . dust, brother, dust! The man looked at him and he laughed.

Jack said, 'In the name of God, who are you? You're bound to be the Devil!'

He says, 'Jack, that's who I am, I'm the Devil.'

'Well,' Jack said, 'look, if you're the Devil, that Devil's money. And it's nae good to me.'

70

'Oh aye, Jack,' he said, 'it's good to you, Jack. You can have as much o' it as you can tak. *But you've got to tak it the way that I canna tak it.*'

Jack looked down and he seen the cloven foot sittin, the right foot, split foot. Jack said, 'If I can lift it the way you canna lift it, can I keep it?'

'That's the bargain, Jack!' he said.

Jack says, 'Right.' Slipped off his old boot, brother, off with his old stocking. He lifted the lid of the box. Jack put the foot into the box, with his two shoes he lifted a gold piece and he put it in his hand. There it was shiny as could be – he put it in his pocket. Another yin. And another yin, till he had about forty. Weight in his pocket. 'Now,' he says to the Devil, 'you do the same for me!'

Devil put the . . . 'No,' says Jack, 'the same foot as me, the right foot – get it in the box and get them out!'

Devil put the cloven foot into the box, brother! He tried with the split foot, but na! Ye're wise! He says, 'Jack, ye finally beat me!' And just like that there were a *flash o' flame*, brother dear! And darkness.

Jack rubbed his eyes, he wakened up. He was sitting with his back against the clift, sober as a judge against the clift. And the clift was closed, not a soul to be seen. He got up, he lifted his mother's wee bundle and he walked home. He landed in, his old mother was sitting in the house.

She said, 'Ye're hame, Jack.'

He said, 'Aye, I'm hame.'

She said, 'Did ye get a wee drink?'

'Drink!' he said, 'Mother, I got mair than a drink . . . I got the biggest fright I ever got in my life.'

'What happened?'

He said, 'I met the Devil!'

'Aye,' she says, 'you met the Devil!'

71

'Aye, I met the Devil,' and he told her the story I'm telling you. 'But, Mother,' he said, 'I beat him, I beat the Devil. He couldna do what I done. You used to cry me, Mother, a lazy cratur when I was sittin at the fire puttin peats on the fire wi my feet.'

'Aye,' she said, 'naebody would put peats on with their feet. It's only you a bundle of laziness!'

'Well,' he said, *'that's* no bundle o' laziness – forty gold sovereigns in my pocket. The Devil couldna lift them with his right foot, but I beat him when I lifted them with mine.' Jack and his mother had forty gold sovereigns, and they had a good time o' it. All because he put the peats in the fire with his foot!

THE CHALLENGE

Now my story takes you back a long time ago to a village in the north of Scotland. It was served by the local community, all farming folk, who came from outlying regions and hill farms. And in this small village there was only one inn where the farmers and shepherds and ploughmen came for a drink on a Saturday evening. At the end of the village was the churchyard that served the whole community. Not only were the people who died in the village buried in the churchyard, but also the farmers of the outlying regions were buried in this cemetery.

So they gathered one evening in the inn. Farmers, shepherds, hill workers, peat cutters came in for their usual week-end at the pub. And they stood there and they had their drinks, they had their talks and they discussed many wonderful things. One by one they all finally moved away to go back to their homes. But there were about a dozen of them left. And the subject they were discussing was the graveyard outside the village, how many people were buried in the cemetery, how long had the people been buried in it, how old it really was. And then someone spoke up and said, 'How about the ghost?'

And they said, 'The ghost?' Oh, everyone knew of the ghost. Many people in the village had reported seeing a ghost at the gate of the graveyard many nights. Many people had seen it, but nobody would believe them.

But in the bar was a girl named Margaret. Now Margaret was a shepherdess who worked for a local farmer. And she was as good as any man – she could clip a sheep as quick as any man, cowp a sheep on its back and clip it, she could cut peats, she could do anything. She was neither feart o' God, man, or the Devil! And they respected her. She was just a young unmarried woman. She was as strong as any man. And she was one of the last ones left in the pub, discussing with the men about the local cemetery.

So the subject got around about the ghost. And it was the owner of the inn who spoke up, 'I bet ye there's not one among yese would even go to the graveyard at twelve o'clock! Yese are all standing there talking about it. But the're not one among yese who would go up to the graveyard and even view the ghost close up!'

Then up spoke Maggie. She said, 'Look, mister,' she said to the pub owner, 'look, mister, I'm not feart o' neither ghost, man or the Devil. And I'll go to the graveyard, and if the're a ghost there I'll wait. And if it comes I'll tell ye what I'll do wi ye, I'll bring you back his shroud or his cloth that he keeps himself white with – we all ken a spirit or a ghost needs something to cover him to keep white – it's no his skeleton folk sees! I'll go up and I'll bring it back to ye. I'll put it on the bar, then will you believe it?'

'No,' he says, 'no, Maggie, no way. Please, don't do it, we're only makin fun!'

She says, 'Look, yese are all supposed to be brave men. Ye're all supposed to be great heroes, among the whole crowd o' yese, while yese hae got a drink in yese. But I'm no a man, but I'm no feart o' God, man or the Devil. And I'll go tonight providin you keep the pub open till after twelve o'clock. And if the're a ghost there, if he's standing at the gate, and if he has a shroud or a sheet on him – I'll bring it back to ye. And fling it ower yer bar!'

74

'Well,' he said, 'Maggie, if that's the way ye want it, I'll tell ye, I'll mak it better for ye. I'll mak a wager wi ye. If the're such a thing as men hae been reportin about, and if you see a ghost and you bring it back – his shroud to me – and put it on the bar, I'll mak it worth your while. I'll gie ye five guinneas and a bottle o' whisky to yersel!'

She says, 'Done!'

So they sat there and they drank, and the clock on the wall said a quarter to twelve. Now in these bygone times the inn owners could keep their pubs open the whole night through, as long as there were people standing to drink. So she said 'good-bye' to them at the bar and she walked up to the graveyard gate. And she stood. She heard the clock in the village striking twelve o'clock as she stood at the gate.

And then across from the gate she saw something white standing with a long shroud on it. And being Maggie, who was neither feart o' God, man, beast or the Devil, she walked up and said, 'Ye're the ghost that's frightening everybody aren't ye? Well, ye canna frighten me.' And she catcht the cloot that was ower him, a white shroud, and she pulled it off him. And she put it under her oxter. There he stood in front o' her, a naked skeleton, nothing but the bones. And she turned her back on him, she walked onwards.

As she's walking on he's coming behind her step after step saying, '*Thoir dhomh air ais mo léine*, oh I'm cold, give me my sheet, give me my sheet. Give me my sheet, I'm cold!'

She said, 'Ye'll get nae sheet from me.' And on she walked.

And he walked on after her. 'Oh, gie me my sheet,' he was crying. '*Thoir dhomh air ais mo léine*, give me my sheet, I'm cold, I'm cold, give me back my sheet.'

So they walked on till they came to the inn. And the door of the inn was open. And he was coming closer and closer to her . . . by this time she began to get kind o' feart that there was

75

really something behind her terrible. And she couldna stand his voice any longer.

He was saying, '*Thoir dhomh air ais mo léine*, give me my sheet, I'm cold!'

And she seen the lights. Now by this time she was feart! Really feart, terrified. But she still kept the sheet under her oxter. And she came up to the door of the inn. And she couldna stand it any longer, 'Well,' she says, 'ye've followed me far enough – there's yer sheet!'

Now, he had no power to touch her till he got his sheet back. But as quick as you could draw a breath he picked up that sheet, wrapped it round him and as she was disappearing inside the door of the inn – and the last part of her was her foot going in through the door – he came down on her foot with his hand! He cut her heel, the last part to disappear into the light, and cut the heel off her.

And she staggered into the inn and collapsed before all the people in the inn. And they rushed round her. There was her heel cut completely off as if it had been done with a knife. This woman was Maggie, she was a herdswoman, a powerful woman, who was as powerful as any man. She sat there in silent agony with her heel gone. So they asked her what happened, and she told them the story. She'd pulled the sheet from the wreft, or the skeleton. And she told them it had followed her to the inn. And she couldna withstand it any longer, she had to throw him the sheet.

And they said, 'Why didn't you bring the sheet in, and he would never hae touched ye.' But that was her mistake. Anyhow, she got her five guinneas and the bottle of whisky. And a cart and horse came to take her back to the farm where she lived.

But after that, that great Maggie, the woman who was as powerful as any man, who could clip sheep, dig drains, do anything, who was neither feart o' God or man or the Devil, just sat there in her chair, a cripple for three months. Never able to do another thing. And then three months later she was found hung by the neck in the farmer's barn. She hung herself on a rope. And the story went on, when people reported later when they came to the pub, let it be true or a lie, that sometimes when they were passing by the gate of the graveyard coming home, let them be drunk or sober, they saw the reflection of not one white thing standing at the gate of the graveyard, but two.

THE MINISTER AND THE DEVIL

It all began a long time ago in a little village in the north of Scotland. The local minister had died and was buried in the cemetery with the people. And then another minister came to take his place, he and his sister came to live in the manse. There wasn't a large population in the village, and after a few months the minister, who was in his forties became well respected. He had never married and his sister Margaret was the only person he ever had any love for in his life. And after a year had passed, one day his sister took ill. She had visits from the local doctor but nothing seemed to help her. She just lay in bed as if in a coma, sick and ill. All the people in the village came to visit her, brought her flowers and things like that. But the minister was very sad because he loved his sister more than anything in the world. Every time as he sat in his little office before he went to bed at night he would pray for the health and welfare of his sister. But to no avail. She never seemed to get any better.

Then one Sunday after he came home from the sermon, he sat in his chair in his little office room in the manse. He said to himself, 'I know to my ownself that my sister is dying. And I've prayed to God many many times to help her, but he has never answered my prayers. I love my sister dearly. God does not seem to want to help me. Maybe the Devil would help me . . . I would go to Hell for my sister!'

And then a voice spoke beside him and said, 'Is it true? Would you really go to Hell for your sister?'

The minister looked around his little room. There stood a tall dark man with a long dark cloak reaching to the floor. And the minister said, 'Who are you, stranger?'

He said, 'Well, you asked for help didn't you? I am the Devil. And I can help your sister.'

'I've prayed to God,' said the minister, 'for many weeks and he doesn't seem to help. But could you really help my sister?'

And the Devil said, 'Yes, I could, I could make her well!' The Devil looked around, he said, 'You have a lovely place here.' The little room was stacked with books, Bibles and hymn books and everything. 'But,' he said, 'it's not like my home. If you would like to come with me for a night – I'll help your sister.'

And the minister said, 'I'll do anything to help my sister, I'll even go to Hell!'

'Well,' said the Devil, 'let's be on our way!'

So the minister said, 'Lead the way!' Now his sister she lay upstairs in bed in a kind of coma. So he said, 'How long will we be gone?'

'Oh, just a short while,' said the Devil, 'just a short while. But be prepared for the things you will see.'

So the minister put on his coat and he and the Devil walked through the door. The Devil led him down to the end of the village. Then he came to a forest that the minister had never seen before. He said to himself, 'There's no forest here.'

But the Devil walked on. The Devil said, 'Follow my footsteps.' And the minister walked on behind the Devil.

Then after they came to the end of the forest they came to a moor. And it was covered in thick brambles! With thorns as thick as your finger. And the Devil walked on through the Moor of Thorns, through a path, and the minister walked behind him. As the minister looked the thorns were closing behind him, and he said to himself, 'I'm bound for Hell. But how will I ever get back?'

So they travelled on and travelled on through the Moor of Thorns, and the thorns closed behind them as they walked. Then, after passing the moor, they came to a flat plain. And the Devil said, 'Be careful now! Put your foot in my footsteps.' Now the Devil had a cloven hoof on one foot and a boot on the other. And it was very hard for the minister to keep in touch with the Devil as he walked along. Now they came to a narrow path that led through a swamp, and the Devil said to the minister, 'Be careful! If you step off this path you will never be seen again! And you'll never get where we're going.' So the minister walked on the little narrow path that led through a steamy hot swamp of bubbling muck and earth, coming bubbling up. And the mist was coming down. The minister slipped his foot – his two legs went into the swamp! The Devil turned round and he put his hand on the minister's shoulder, he picked him up as if he was a feather and put him straight on the path. 'Now,' he said, 'I told you to be careful!' The minister was covered in slime and green muck to the knees. But they travelled on till the end of the path. Then they came to a large dark cavern. 'Don't be afraid,' says the Devil, 'just follow me!'

So he led in through a dark long passage through a cavern, and the minister could hear the drip and drip and drip of water falling from above. But after a certain length of time they came to an opening at the end – there was bright lights and torches shining on a wall in this great open cavern. And hanging on the wall were hundreds and thousands of skeletons! There were skeletons lying on the floor, there were heads lying here, there were feet lying there, hands lying here. The minister said to himself, 'There must be half o' the people in the world here!' But they still walked on.

'Come!' says the Devil.

But the minister says, 'Where are we?'

The Devil said, 'We're just approaching Hell.'

So they travelled on through the large tunnel, and when they came to the end there was a great open room that was lit with torches blazing from the wall. There was a great burning fire in front of the open chamber.

'Come up,' said the Devil, 'to the fire!'

And the minister walked behind the Devil to the fire. There was a great flagstone, and a burning bright fire that never seemed to burn down. But two iron chairs were on each side of the fireplace. And in one chair sat an old man with a long grey beard, he was smiling away as if he was smiling in his sleep. Around the wall were all these people tied with chains around their necks.

And the Devil said, 'Do you see anyone you recognise?'

The minister walked all around. There were farmers he had met, people who had come to his church . . . there was an old man with grey hair sitting on a chair with spikes. And a bag made of leather hanging above him with a hole in the bag of water – it was 'drip, drip, drip' on his head. And he was sitting there waiting for every drip that fell. 'That is the minister who was in church before me!' said the minister.

'I know,' said the Devil, 'he was fond of putting holy water on people's heads. Now he will have water on *his* head to the end of eternity!'

And then he walked up to the fire, there was a man hanging by his feet with his head above the fire. The minister looked, it was the village doctor who had recently died, and whom he'd said a sermon for. 'That's the village doctor!' said the minister.

'Of course,' said the Devil, 'he's the village doctor. And he cured too many people! He always loved to tell them to keep warm and stay by their fires, so now *he* will hang by the fire to the end of eternity!'

'Now,' says the Devil, 'I welcome you to my home! But before I introduce you to the rest of my people I have something to do.'

And the minister looked around. There were cages all along the wall. In the cages were these ugly little imps with their long skinny nails and ugly faces. They were biting and scratching each other.

'Oh,' the Devil looked when he saw the minister watching, he said, 'These are my imps, these are my workers! So just a moment, before we start anything else let me feed my friends.' And sitting by the fireside was a great pot of boiling lead. In the pot was a large ladle. And the Devil went over, he took a boiling ladleful and he started, he said, 'It's nice when you've got to feed them. Open your mouths!' and he passed to every one who was chained to the wall. And they opened their mouths. The Devil put a heap of boiling lead in their mouths. He said, 'Isn't it nice when it sizzles in their throats!'

The minister stood there transfixed and aghast. He saw his old friend the carpenter. He saw his old friend the blacksmith. He saw many old friends, the farmers opening their mouths and getting ladles of boiling lead.

'Listen,' said the Devil, 'do you hear it sizzle in their throats? But soon they will be gone!'

Then the minister said, 'What do you mean?'

'Well,' he said, 'soon my imps will come and tear their bodies asunder. And I will retain my lead when it cools in their stomachs and put it back in the pot. And they will join my skeletons in my passage. Isn't it wonderful when the wind blows through, when their bones rattle, isn't it music!'

And the poor minister stood there, he was transfixed, he said, 'What kind of place is this I am in? This is really Hell!'

So after the Devil had served all his patients who hanged to the wall, he said, 'I have someone to show you.'

But the minister looked – there still sitting by the fireside was an old man with a grey beard smiling away to himself. The minister said, 'I know him!'

'Of course,' said the Devil, 'you know him! He is the village drunkard. And he has a place of honour by my fireside. He had broken every rule in the land. He was a thief and a cheat and a drinker. They condemned him in the village. He had done more evil in his life than anyone I can think of, and he is my special guest!'

But the minister looked . . . there was an empty chair by the fire on the other side.

'Come,' said the Devil, 'I have something special to show you. Come and meet my mother!'

So they passed through a small channel into another room which was brightly lit. And the Devil led him in, there was another burning fire! And on a flagstone sat an old woman, the most evil looking creature that the minister had ever seen in his life!

He said, 'That's my mother.'

She had three toes that were covered in hair, she was dressed in a long black dress that was actually made of something like moss, and it came to the floor. She had peaked ears and lumps and warts on her face. Her teeth were overlapping and rotting and her gums were moulding. And her two eyes were blazing from her head!

Beside her sat a large iron pot. She was putting her hand into the iron pot bringing up toads, live toads and frogs, and spearing them with a piece of stick and holding them on the fire. The minister stood there terrified, as he watched the old woman holding a toad in the fire till its wee legs stretched out and its eyes bulged with the heat and its mouth opened. And when she thought it was half cooked, she put it in her mouth, she started to cr-r-unch the bones and swallow the toad. You could see that she only had three fingers on each hand and

84

her nails and the backs of her hands were covered in hair, and her nails were like nails of cats. The minister stood and gazed in amazement because beside her was a large black snake, the largest black snake he had ever seen in his life. And sometiomes she would dip her hand into the pot and put a frog in the snake's mouth, and the snake would swallow the frog.

The Devil spoke up and said to his mother, 'Mother, I have brought someone to see you.'

And her eyes opened and she stood up.

The Devil said, 'Mother, are you listening? I have brought someone to see you!' And he turned to the minister and said, 'She's a little deaf. I think she's eating too many frogs. Too many toads is the cause of the trouble, I'll have to change her diet and get her some snakes or some serpents or some rats.'

And then the old woman came up and stood in front of the minister. Her eyes were blazing and her three-toed fingers were curled in front of the minister – the minister stepped back!

And the Devil said, 'Don't worry, she will not touch you. Don't be afraid. She is very harmless. She never had her drink yet.' He went to a stone shelf and he took a stone bottle. He carried it over, 'Mother,' he said, 'sit down and I'll give you your drink!'

The old woman started to drink from the bottle, and the blood began to run over her chin. And the snake came up from the table and began to lick the blood from her chin with its forked tongue!

And the Devil turned to the minister and said, 'It's only bats' blood. What do you think of my mother?'

The minister stood there aghast, he had never seen such a thing in his life.

And the Devil took the stone bottle from his mother. He put it back on the shelf. 'Now,' he said, 'sit down there, Mother, by the fire!'

'And now,' said the Devil to the minister, 'come with me!'

And he led him round through another channel into a smaller room with a great burning fire. There by the fire was a stone bed and a stone table. And on the table lay about twenty bats with their throats cut, and a heap of mushrooms. The Devil popped a mushroom in his mouth. 'That's my supper,' he said, 'my mother gets the blood and I get the bats! Now, minister, what do you think of all this?'

The minister stood there and he was shaking in fright. He was terrified. Never in his life had he believed that there were such a thing.

'Now,' he said, 'you've come to visit me and I've come to visit you, minister. But remember . . .'

The minister said, 'I want to go home to my own place.'

'You will go home,' said the Devil. 'But someday you will be back. Because you see I have a place for you, if you do what I tell you.'

'What have I got to do?' said the minister.

'Give up your ministry,' he said. 'Because preaching "good" will never help you in Hell!'

'Please,' said the minister, 'I want to go back!'

'You want to go back?' said the Devil. 'Well, you'll go back,' and then the Devil snapped his fingers and there was a blaze of sparking light!

The minister closed his eyes because he could not look at the light. And then when he opened his eyes . . . he was back in his own room. And his sister Margaret was standing with a candle and a cup o' tea.

She says, 'John, I have brought you a cup o' tea.'

And the minister was amazed, he said, 'Sister, you're well!'

'Of coure I'm well!' she said. 'John, what happened to you? Have you fallen asleep in your chair?' And she looked down, she said, 'John, where have you been?' And his legs to the knees were covered in dried sticky *evil mud*.

He said, 'Sister, I have been in Hell.'

And from that day on the minister went and gave up his church. He resigned from the church the next morning. He collected at the Bibles and hymn books he could find in the manse, he went out to the back yard, he heaped them up and he set them on fire. He moved into a little cottage in the village. There he lived with his old sister – a healthier woman you could never find. And he became a drunk, he broke every rule in the Bible. He drank and he spent, spent every penny he could find. And one evening after a number of years had passed, when the local minister had become the town drunk, he was found dead in the churchyard. So they buried him and gave him a lovely sermon.

And back in Hell the two seats by the Devil's fire are filled. In one of them is the village drunk who sits and smiles as he watches the Devil giving lead to all the people who come to Hell. But he has no fear because he is the Devil's special friend. And in the other seat sits someone else, I'm sure you know who he is! And that is the end of my story.

THE TRAMP AND THE FARMER

It was very late when the old beggar-man came to the rich farmyard. He had travelled far that day, he was tired and hungry. He said to himself, 'I must find somewhere to sleep,' because it was snowing. There were many buildings in this farm by the side-road. He said, 'I will go up here, maybe the farmer will help me. He has many barns, he has many sheds. He could probably give me somewhere to lie down.' So the old beggar-man walked up to the farmhouse and he knocked on the door.

The farmer was just after finishing his tea, and his wife said, 'There's someone at the door.'

And the farmer said, 'Well, I'll go and see who's there.' He walked out and there at his door stood an old beggar-man with his old grey hair and his old ragged coat. He had travelled for many miles. And the farmer said, 'What do you want, old man?'

He said, 'Please, sir, I'm just an old beggar. Would you, please, could you help me?'

'What do you want of me?' said the farmer.

'Look, just a shed,' he said, 'or a barn or any place you could let me lie for the night. It's a cold night and it's snowing. I'm hungry and tired, but just a place to lie down would be enough for me for the night. Just some place to shelter.'

And the farmer said, 'You're a beggar! Old man, I need my barns for my cattle. The woods are fit for you. Go and sleep in the wood, old man, we shelter no beggars here. My barns are for my cattle, not for you, old beggar-man. Go and sleep in the wood! This is not for you!'

The old beggar just turned around. He said, 'I'm sorry, sir.' And he walked away. The farmer closed his door.

But the courtyard of the farm was a big yard. And there were two ways leading from the yard, the road leading up to the farm and the road leading away from the farm. The old beggar walked among the snow coming down. And who at that moment was coming out from a shed but the farmer's coachman. In these days it was all horses and coaches, and there was a special shed made for the coaches. The man was just after cleaning up the farmer's coach, his special coach that took him to the village and to the town. He had put the coach in the shed. And when he walked out the first person he met was the old beggar-man, who was walking down through the farmyard.

The coachman said, 'Where are you going, old man?'

And the old beggar said, 'I was up at the farmer, son. I was lookin for a shelter for the night, an' I asked him to let me sleep in the barn or any shed he had, any shed, just for shelter from the snow. And he told me to go and sleep in the woods.'

'O-oh,' said the coachman, 'you cannot sleep in the woods, old beggar-man. It's too cold tonight. Let me help you.'

'Your master will be angry,' said the old beggar.

'Never mind my master,' said the coachman. 'Come with me, one place I will take you to where he will never find you. Come into my coach-shed. I have just cleaned up the farmer's coach. Come with me, old beggar, and the farmer will never find you there!'

And he took him into the coach-shed, he opened up one of the farmer's prize coaches. He said, 'Old beggar-man, it is comfortable in there. Go to sleep in there. Be out early in the morning and no-one will ever know you've been there!' So he put the old beggar in and he closed the door – a beautiful leather coach, all done up in beautiful leather. And the old beggar-man stretched himself out and went to sleep. The coachman went home to his wife and family.

The farmer inside the house went to bed. He went to sleep. But as he lay in bed and went to sleep, he had a dream. He dreamt that he died and he went to Hell. And when he landed in Hell all the people that he knew in his life-time, who had died before him, were all sitting round waiting their turn.

There was the Devil standing with a big pot of boiling lead and a ladle in his hand. And all the people round, all whom he had known who had died and he'd met in the market many years before, farmers he had known for many years were all sitting round waiting their turn. One by one they were called up, and the Devil took a ladle of boiling lead. They opened their mouths and they swallowed it, and they were suffering in pain and they called in pain! One by one till it came his turn. And the Devil beckoned him up, 'Come,' he said, 'farmer! It's your turn next!' And the Devil put the ladle in, in his pot of lead and said to the farmer, 'Open your mouth! It's your turn!'

The farmer opened his mouth and the Devil put a ladleful of boiling lead in his mouth. And he felt it going down in his throat, it was burning him, it was burning in his throat and it was burning in his chest. And he said, 'O-oh God! What have I done for this? If only I had one sip of water to cool my mouth!'

Then he looked up. And there came an old beggar-man with two brass cans of water before him. He stood before the farmer. The farmer said, 'Please, I beg of you! Please! Old

91

beggar-man, please, please, I beg of you! Please, my mouth is burning, my throat is burning. Please give me one . . . even put your finger in, put one dreep on my tongue to cool my mouth!'

The old beggar-man said, 'No. My master forbids me. I cannot give you one sip. No more than you could give me one night's sleep in your barn.' And then the old beggar-man was gone.

'O-o-oh,' said the farmer, 'what have I done for this? Please, what have I done for this?' And then he wakened up in his bed. 'O-oh God,' he said to himself, 'what have I done? What have I done? That old beggar that's in . . . that old beggar is probably in my barns, probably he's smokin, probably he's lightin his pipe an settin my barns on fire!' He got up from his bed.

He walked round all the sheds on his farm. But he never saw the old beggar. Then he saw a light in the coach-house. He walked down, an' he opened the door of the coach-house. Then he walked into the coach and he saw the old beggar lying there — *four hands holding two candles each beside the old beggar's head and at his feet.* And the farmer was aghast. He walked back, backwards from the shed. He said, 'It's the old beggar and he's dead. He walked home, he went to his bed. But he never had another dream.

Next morning when he got up he called for the coachman. The coachman came before him. He said, 'Coachman, did you let an old beggar in my coach last night?'

The coachman said, 'Yes, master. You can sack me if you want to. I don't care. You can have my job. But I could not let an old beggar lie asleep in the snow.'

And the farmer said to him, 'Sack you? My man, I'm not going to sack you in any way. I'm going to make you manager of my farm and everything I own, you can work it for me for the rest of your life! Tomorrow morning I want you to go down to the joiners and get a beautiful sign made telling the world – Tramps and Beggars will be Welcome – and a bed and whatever they can eat. Put it at my road-end. And you can run the farm for me for the rest of my time.'

So the coachman got that done. He put a sign on the roadside at the farm saying Tramps and Beggars will be Welcome. But the farmer waited, and he waited and he waited for many many years. Never a tramp or a beggar ever came to his doorway until the day he died. And what happened to that farmer I'm sure you know as well as what I do.

THE MILLER AND THE DEVIL

Once upon a time there lived a miller many many years ago. He was a good miller and he worked hard, he milled well. He milled all the corn round the village and the district where he stayed. And he had one daughter. His wife had died when the baby was very young. But she was always down upon him, because he worked hard all week and he always went to an inn on the week-end for a drink. And he'd go home well under the weather. His daughter would take him and put him to bed, and he'd say 'I'm the finest, the greatest miller in the country. I can mill anyone's meal! I can mill, I can make flour and meal as good as any miller – I can even make flour fit for the Devil!' And he always had this habit o' saying these very words every time he got a wee drink.

But one day he was up to his eyes in work. Farmers were bringing their loads of corn to get milled, and the miller was stacked to his very eyes with bags of corn. Now these old-time mills were watermills. They had a big dam and the water turned the mill wheel. When the wheel turned round with the force of water, it drove the mill and bruised the corn, made the meal and made the flour – all by a dam fed by a wee brook at the back of the mill. The miller was hard at work this day when in comes this man with a bag on his back, a black bag full of corn.

'Good morning, miller,' says he.

'Oh, good morning,' says the miller. 'What can I do for ye?'

'Well,' he says, 'I want you to make me a bag of flour, the best o' white flour.'

'Well,' he says, 'I'll make you a bag of my best flour. But you'll have to wait.'

'Oh no,' says the man, 'I canna wait.'

'Why no?' says the miller to this man.

'I need it right away,' he says, 'I need a bag of flour. Or half a bag, whatever you can manage.'

'Well,' he says, 'what have you got?'

He said, 'I've got a bag of corn.'

'Well,' he says, 'a bag of corn disna make a bag of flour. A bag o' corn'll make half a bag of flour.'

'Well,' he says, 'half a bag of flour will do.'

'But,' he says, 'you'll have to wait. There's Mr Bain, Mr Munro and all the other farmers, all their bags is sittin waitin to get milled. And you'll have to wait. Come back.'

'No,' says the man, 'I canna come back. I want ye to make my bag right away.'

He says, 'I can't do it.'

He says, 'Ye'll have to do it. Because I'm needin it right now!'

'I can't do it,' he said.

He said, 'You'll do it!'

Now the miller began to get a wee bit upset, 'No,' he said, 'I won't do it!'

'Oh,' says the man, 'you'll do it, ye'll do it for me right now!'

The miller says, 'Over my dead body tonight! I wouldna make nobody's meal, nobody's flour till I get everything done that I've already laid out for to do. You are no entitled, yours is no entitled to be done any more than anybody else's. Over my dead body!'

'*So be it,*' said the man, '*over your dead body . . . it could be done.*' And he left his black bag down on the floor, and away he went.

Now it was right raining. The old miller stopped the mill, and he went into his house. His daughter was keeping house for him.

She says, 'Daddy, do you want your tea?'

'No,' he says, 'I dinna want nae tea.'

She said, 'You've been workin hard today. You've been workin very hard, Father.'

'Well,' he said, 'no nae harder than any other day. But I feel terrible funny, I think I'll go to my bed and lie down.' Now this is a queer thing for the miller to do because when he came in he usually came to his daughter, had his tea, sat and had a wee drink, and he talked. He was a cheery miller, and his daughter and him were quite happy. They had everything under the sun that they needed. But he went straight, right to his bed.

His daughter came in and asked him, 'Are ye wantin . . .'

But no answer.

'Och,' she said, 'my daddy's prob'ly tired. He'll prob'ly no be wantin nae supper tonight. He must be workin hard.'

So the next morning she went in. Father wasna up. She says, 'Daddy, ye gettin up?'

No answer.

She pulled back the blankets. And her daddy was lying, just lying staring, not asleep, not awake, his two eyes just staring as if he was dead. That's all she saw, just the movement of his eyes. So the lassie was very worried, she shook him, she inspected him, she helped him up, did everything. No move, no movement of any description. Just as if he was dead. He looked up at her, but he couldna speak, couldna move, couldna do nothing. The lassie was terrible terrible worried. She was fair upset, she didna ken what to do. She went back down, she walked round the house, she couldna do no housework or nothing, she was upset about her daddy.

But no far away from the mill, in fact about three mile away, lived an old woman and her son Jack who had a wee croft. And the old woman said to her son, 'Jack, now we've got the harvest finished, I wonder would you tak that wee puckle corn along to the miller and get it thrashed? And get us enough oatmeal for to make some bannocks and porridge to keep me and you, to do us ower the winter?' Jack's father had died when he was very young and they didna hae any horses. A donkey they had, and a wee cart.

'Well, Mother,' he said, 'I'm no doin very much. Before the long winter nights come, I think I'll take your wee puckle corn along to the mill, see how the old miller's gettin on. I'll get him to thrash it for ye, an' I'll bring back the meal.' Now ten bags of corn makes about fourteen to fifteen bags of meal when it's thrashed.

So Jack had a wee donkey and a wee cart and he packed the ten bags in his wee cart, he yoked up his donkey and he went along to the mill leading his donkey, his cuddy, by the head. And he landed at the mill. The mill was silent. 'Man,' he said, 'I wonder how the old miller . . .' Now Jack was well acquainted with the miller and well acquainted with the miller's daughter in the town. 'I wonder what happened to the old miller,' he said. 'Maybe he's sick, maybe the're something wrong with him. I wonder what's really wrong.'

He goes round, takes his wee cuddy cart round the back of the mill. There's a big round open door going in to the mill wheel. The dam is full. The wheel is quiet. And he has to go down three steps, and down a wee passage to the door. Jack stops his donkey at the big open door going in to the mill. All the bags belonging to the other people are sitting on the floor.

98

He leads the donkey down, he knocks at the door. And the lassie comes out. 'Hello!' he says to her.

'Hello, John,' she said, 'hello!'

He says, 'What's wrong?'

'It's my daddy,' she said, 'he's no very well. In fact. I don't know what's wrong wi him.'

He said, 'What happened?'

'Well,' she said, 'I don't know what happened. Yesterday he came in, he'd been working hard and he came in and he went straight to bed. He's lying there, not asleep . . . as if he's alive and no more.'

'Did ye call any of them doctor folk?' he said.

She said, 'I called the doctor man and he cam and he had a look at him. And he's in some kind o' coma, some kind o' deep sleep. The're nothing in the world they can do for him.'

'God bless me,' said Jack, 'that's queer. Had he ever been troubled like that before?'

'No,' she said, 'ye ken what like my father is, he's never been troubled before. And that's no it – God knows how long he'll be like that! All the farmers round about the country is cryin for their corn to get thrashed. And I dinna ken one thing about the mill. I dinna ken a soul in the country that could help me!'

'Ah,' says Jack, 'I'll tell ye the truth, I'm no doin very much. I'm willin to help ye, as much as I can.'

'Oh,' she says, 'Jack, that would be an awfa good thing, if you could help me, even if you could get the mill goin, thrash some o' that stuff that's left and get it through to the farmers. Try and clean up the backlog o' stuff that's lyin. And you could prob'ly do your ain forbyes. How many bags hae you got?'

He said, 'I've ten.'

'Oh well,' she said, 'that'll take a bit o' doin. I dinna ken what's wrong wi my father, I'm awfa worried about him.'

'Well,' Jack said, 'I'll tell ye, I'll leave my bags o' corn. I canna start today. I'll come back and I'll take my cuddy and cart hame, and stead my donkey. I'll walk back and the first thing in the morning, I'll start the mill. I'll thrash it and I'll thrash all day, I'll mill all what's in there – it'll maybe be a wee help to ye.'

'All right, Jack,' she says, 'I'm very much obliged to ye and I thank ye very much,' said the old miller's daughter.

So Jack empties his cart, puts his bags sitting on the floor. And sitting in the one corner was a wee black bag. Jack looks. He says, 'I wonder who brought that in, a black bag.' It was a pure black burlap bag. 'Well, upon my soul,' he says, 'I've never seen a bag like that before. I wonder what's in it.' And it was tied with a string. He opened the bag, and he put his hand in and he looked – it was pure bottle-black corn, real black corn. 'Well, upon my soul,' he said, 'I've heard o' it, but this is the first time I've ever seen it.' Now very few people has ever seen black corn. He put the handful o' corn back in the bag and he tied it.

He turns his wee donkey and back he goes to his mother. His old mother is waiting on him coming back.

She says, 'Ye're back early, Jack, what happened?'

'Well, Mother, to tell ye the truth,' he said, 'I never got nae meal. The miller is no well.'

'God bless me,' she said, 'what's wrong?'

'Well seemingly, as far as I'm led to believe,' he said, 'the lassie tellt me today that her father came in fae his work yesterday, and he never took any supper. He went straight to his bed and he lay down.'

'Oh,' she said, 'that's very rare. He's a hard workin man, and a healthier man you never saw in your life. What can be doin wi him?'

'Well, Mother,' he said, 'his daughter disna ken what can be doin wi him, because the're something funny wrong wi

100

him. He's lyin in bed and he's as good as deid. And the lassie's awfa upset. I promised the morn I'd go back and start the mill, and mill all the taste o' corn and grain that's left for her, to gie her a wee help out.'

The old woman said, 'Did she no get some o' these doctors, these quack folk up and see what's wrong wi him?'

'Aye,' he said, 'the lassie done her best for him. But he's just lyin there as if he's deid.'

'Well,' the old woman said, 'Jack, it's a good thing ye're goin back to help. God bless me, it's funny . . . I kent him all the days of my life, an' a healthier man ye never seen. Maybe he took a stroke or something. Onyway, if you gang along the morn to do the wee bit work, maybe I should gang along wi ye. Tak a couple eggs and a drop fresh milk along to the lassie onyway. In fact, I haena been to the mill for a long while, I would like to go along.'

'Mother,' he said, 'if it's no puttin you out o' the way – I'll be there all day. It'll prob'ly be late before I'm back.'

'Ah,' she says, 'what have I got here? The're nothing here for me when you're awa. The best thing I can do, I'll pack my wee basket and I'll go along wi ye in the mornin.'

So naturally the day passed by and morning came, as the story tells, Jack got up and had his bit breakfast, yoked his donkey. And he and the old woman made their way towards the mill. So they landed at the mill, Jack loosed his donkey out, put it in the wee paddock in the front of the mill and shoved his wee cart aside. And his old mother went into the house and so did he. The lassie came out.

'God bless me, lassie,' the woman said, 'Jack tellt me last night that yer poor father is no very well! What happened to him?'

'I dinna ken,' she says, 'what happened to him. Ever* he came in fae his work he kept mumbling for a while about some man wi a bag of corn, but that's all I can get out o' him.

* ever - continually from the time

101

Some man cam wi a bag o' corn. That's all that happened. But it's thankin God to be praised that yer son Jack has come today to gie me a wee help out. See if maybe in a couple o' days my father'll maybe come to hissel, I'm awfa worried about him.'

'Well I cam along the day,' she said, 'I could be a bit help to ye. I'll go in and see yer father onyway.' So the old woman, Jack's mother, went into the house and into the old man's bedroom.

And the old man is lying on his back, his two eyes just staring out looking. Not a murmur, not asleep, not nothing, just his two eyes staring.

'God bless me!' the old woman said. The old woman blessed herself when she came back in. She said, 'Lassie, yer father's in a bad way.'

'Aye,' she said, 'old wife, my father's in a bad way. But I dinna ken what's wrong. I don't know . . . since that day in the mill I don't know what's wrong wi him.'

'Well,' she said, 'I cam here today and the're two-three eggs and some butter I made mysel. If he rallies, comes round about, ye can maybe make a wee taste o' gruel or something for him. But Jack's goin to start the mill up.'

Jack went to the mill. The dam was in beautiful bloom, full of water to the mouth. Beautiful dam of water had gathered for the couple of days that the miller was ill. Jack filled the hopper, put five or six bags o' corn into the hopper, switched on the water. Round goes the big wooden wheel. The waterfall turns the wheel and the wheel turns other wheels inside the mill and these turn a belt, and the belt turns a crusher that bruises the corn and makes it into oatmeal. Or if you want to bruise it further it makes it into flour. So Jack's busy working away. But he hasna worked very long when in comes this man. Tall dark man.

'Good morning, miller,' he says.

Jack says, 'Good morning, but I'm no the miller.'

'Oh-ho, but you're millin aren't ye?'

'Aye,' said Jack, 'I'm millin, but I'm no the miller.'

'Well,' he said, 'have you got my flour?'

Jack says, 'What flour? I have nae flour.'

'Well,' he said, 'there I left my bag the day before yesterday wi the miller. And I want a bag of flour.'

'Well,' Jack said, 'look, I doubt ye'll have to wait for a while for flour, because we're no makin any flour today or I'm no makin any flour. And the miller's ill.'

'Oh,' he said, 'the miller's ill. Oh, I believe the miller's ill.'

'And,' he said, 'I want to help out.' Jack tellt him the story, 'And I'm helpin out the miller, I'm goin to thrash all that, it's goin for meal. But I'm no makin any flour.'

He says, 'I want my flour!'

Jack looks at this man. He was the queerest looking man Jack had ever seen, dark eyebrows meeting together, tall, dark, dark hair, about fifty or sixty years of age. Dark skin, peaked face, dark moustache. Jack looks very queer at him . . . Very dark, very black.

He said, I cam in here day before yesterday wi a bag o' corn, and the miller failed to bruise it for me and make me some flour. I want some flour made! And he said "over his dead body would he make flour to me". But he boasted that he could make flour for the Devil!'

'God bless me,' says Jack, 'I hope you're no the Devil.'

He says, 'You'll never know. But I want you to take my meal, my corn, and put it throught that hopper, make me a bag of flour!'

Jack said, 'It's out of the question. It canna be done. Look, all these bags that's sitting on the floor have got to be done first. If you'd hae come three days ago and your bag was sitting there, I would hae done it for you.'

He said, 'You'll make my bag right now!'

'No,' says Jack, 'I'm no makin your bag right now. Not a fear, I'm no makin your bag right now!'

'Well,' he said, 'if you dinna mak my bag, you dinna mak naebody else's.'

'It's your bag . . . when everybody else's is finished,' he said, 'I'll mak your bag.'

He says, *'My bag or nobody else's!'*

'Well,' Jack said, 'that's okay. I canna do your bag.'

The mill stopped.

Jack looked round. The man was gone. Jack worked the levers, he pulled the belts, he thought it was choked with too much corn, everything else, he emptied the hopper. But no. Mill wouldna work. No way. 'God bless me,' said Jack, 'the mill'll no work. What's happened?' He pulled the levers again, tried, na! The wheel wouldna move, the hoppers wouldna go. 'Maybe,' said Jack, 'the're a choke, maybe the water choked.' Jack went round to the back of the well, and he looked. The miller's dam was dry. Not a sip water o' no description, dry as a whistle. Now Jack said to his ainsel, 'Look, I couldna hae run all the water through the mill, not in that time. Because a miller's dam, a full dam, can run a whole mill for a full fearin day. There must be something happenin. I'll go into the house and see my mother and tell her.'

In he goes, and his mother and the miller's daughter are sitting at the table. He is very worried looking and the old woman can see it, she says 'What's wrong, laddie?' Are ye finished?'

'No,' says Jack, 'I'm no finished. But the mill's finished.'

'How can that be,' she said, 'the mill's finished? Hae you got through all the grain already? Ye havena been workin, it's only been twa hours and dinna tell me ye thrashed the lot!'

'No, Mother,' he said, 'the pond's dry. The dam's dry.'

'Ah, laddie,' she sais, 'that's impossible. The dam canna be dry, that dam can run a mill for a week and never be dry!'

'Mother,' he says, 'wait a minute, you never heard the rest o' the story. I hadna been millin for half an hour after I started when this man cam to the mill.'

'What kind o' man was he?' she said.

'He asked me to mak him a bag o' flour. He persisted and he persuaded, and he said he wanted me to mak his flour in front o' everybody else's grain. And I said I wouldna do it. And he turned round and tellt me, "If ye dinna do mine, then ye dinna do naebody else's." And like that he was gone. And the mill stopped. I went round the back, the pond was dry.'

So the lassie said, 'Wait a minute, Jack. Was that the same man that cam wi the bag o' corn to my father?'

He says, 'What do you mean, cam wi a bag o' corn to your father?'

'Well,' she said, 'before my father went to bed the last day, he said there's a man, a tall black dark man cam here wi a bag of corn on his back.'

Jack said, 'I dinna ken nothin about him. I never heard about this before.'

'Well,' she said, 'he wanted my father to mak him a bag o' flour, white flour. And my father asked him what kind o' corn he had, and he said it was black corn.'

Jack said, 'There's nae much black corn grown about the country nowadays. I've heard my father and my grandfather speakin about it, but naebody bothers nowadays, naebody ever grows it. They believe it's no lucky, it's unholy or evil to grow black corn. Because when ye mill it people think the're a lot o' mouse's dirt among it, and they'll no buy it. Nae miller'll ever mill black corn. It must be something evil attached to black corn.'

105

'Wait a minute,' says the old woman, 'wait a minute, Jack. Tell me your side o' the story. I've got an inklin that there's somethin wrong here.'

'Well,' he says, 'Mother, after I started to mill, this man cam in. An' afore I cam home to you when I left my corn bags the first time, I looked in the corner and there's a black bag sittin. And in that bag is black corn.'

'Aye,' says the lassie, 'Jack that's the bag that the man brung to my father, and wanted my father to make a bag o' flour for him.'

'This is queer,' said the old woman, 'I doubt, there's something wrong here somewhere. Daughter,' she says to the lassie, 'what kind of flour did he want?'

She says, 'He wanted the best of white flour.'

'But wait a minute,' says the old woman, 'there's nae miller breathin can make pure white flour out o' black corn, as far as I'm led to believe. No that I ken much about black corn, but I mind my father and my grandfather tellin me in the olden days. They growed a lot o' black corn in these days, but you couldna mak the best of white flour out o' black corn . . . impossible. But,' she said, 'Jack, how did the dam stop? Did the mill travel fast?'

'No,' says Jack, 'the mill didna travel fast.'

'But,' she said, 'where did the water go?'

Jack said, 'I don't know where the water's gone.'

'Well,' she says, 'Jack, I'll tell ye, the morn I'll gang to the mill. You sit here, I'll go to the mill.'

So the old woman, Jack and the lassie stayed the night in the mill. And the next morning Jack and the lassie sat at the table having their breakfast, and the old woman went to the mill.

She's pullin the levers here and she's pullin levers there, kidding on that she's working! But she never had no sooner come to the mill, kidding on she was working this and

106

sweeping that, when in comes this man. Tall and dark, eyebrows meeting each other. And the old woman looked. She knew, the old woman knew straightaway that this man wasna for good. He was evil.

'Good morning, missus,' he said, 'good morning.'

'Good morning, sir,' she said. 'What can I do for ye?'

'Well,' he said, 'I'm here to see about my flour.'

She says, 'What flour?' Have you ordered, or what flour do ye want?'

He says, 'I left my corn. I left my corn to get milled.'

'Oh aye,' she says, 'ye left yer corn. But the miller's sick.'

'Oh aye,' he says, 'I know the miller's sick. I know the miller's sick.'

'And the man that was here that took the miller's place,' she said, 'the dam went dry. And I canna start the mill.'

'Aha,' he says, 'but they wouldna work. They wouldna work for me.'

'Well,' she said, 'I'm here and I'll work for you. What do you want?'

He says, 'I want a bag of flour.'

'Well,' she said, 'look, there's all that people's stuff lyin there round the floor to be milled. And I'll mak your flour, seein I can run the mill. But we need water.'

'Oh,' he said, 'I'll get you water. As much water as you need.'

'I need all the water,' she says, 'that can turn the mill.'

'Well,' he said, 'I'll turn your mill.'

'But wait a minute,' she says, 'afore you go any further. I'm led to believe you cam here the first time and you met the miller.'

'Aye,' he said, 'I cam here and I met the miller, and I wanted him to mill me a bag o' grain, and mak me a bag o' flour.'

'But,' she says, 'what have you got?'

He said, 'I've got a bag of corn.'

She said, 'What kind o' corn?'

He said, 'It's black corn.'

'Well,' she said, 'what did ye want?'

He says, 'I wanted a bag of white flour made.'

'Now,' she says, 'wait a minute. You ken that there's naebody alive that can mak white flour out o' black corn.'

'Well,' he said, 'he went about the country boastin that *he could mak flour fit for the Devil!* He said he could. I'm the Devil, and I want him to mill me "a bag of flour fit for the Devil". I want a bag o' the best white flour made out of black corn.'

'Well,' she said, 'there's nae man alive . . . But I'm no a man. I'm a woman. But I'll mak ye a bag o' flour – if you turn on the water.'

He says, 'I'll turn on the water.'

'I'll make ye a bag of flour,' she said, 'I'll make ye a bag o' white flour out o' your black corn, but I'm only an old woman. And I'm no fit to lift your bag on to the hopper.' A hopper is a big thing that holds all the grain. Now the hopper was empty and you had to walk up three steps and cowp a bag of corn into the hopper, so's it would pass down through the hopper into the hammer mill that grinds it into dust to make flour. She says, 'You tak your bag o' black corn. Turn on the water, mister, Devil, as you cry yourself, turn on the water and put the mill goin!'

He says, 'You start the mill!'

The old woman pulled the lever, and the mill went. 'Now' she says, 'I'm an old woman. You carry your bag up and put it in the hopper. But there's only one way that you're goin to get your white flour out o' your black corn – *if you put in the last pea first!* Shake in yer corn, but put in the last pea first!'

Devil walked up the steps and he stood above her with his bag in his oxter. He says, 'Curse you, woman, curse ye and curse the mill for evermore!' And like that he went out in a *blaze of light* through the door!

The old woman walked down to the house and she came in. 'Jack!' she said.

He says, 'Mother, what's wrong?'

She says, 'Jack, that was the Devil.'

'What do you mean?' says the daughter.

'Jack, that was the Devil,' she said.

Like that, who comes walking in through the doorway but the old miller! And he's rubbing his eyes, 'God bless me,' he says, 'I had a long sleep.'

'What do you mean,' said the old woman, 'you had a long sleep? You were near death!'

'Aye,' he said, 'I was near death, near death ower the heid o' a silly fool that cam in here wantin me to mak white flour out o' black corn. Naebody in the world could mak white flour out o' black corn, no even me, and I'm the greatest miller in the world!'

'Stop,' says the old woman, 'stop! Dinna say it.'

'Dinna say what?'

'Never again,' she said, 'say, "ye can make flour fit for the Devil"! That was the Devil that cam to ye!'

So Jack and his mother stayed that day at the mill. And Jack helped the old man to mill all that was sitting on the floor. Before all the grain was finished, and before they had squared up, Jack fell in love with the miller's daughter and the miller fell in love with Jack's old mother. And the four o' them got married. Instead o' the Devil bringing bad luck to them, the Devil brung them good luck! And that's the last o' my wee story.

THE HENWIFE AND THE DEVIL

A long time ago an old woman lived all alone in a little cottage by the shoreside. She was a henwife, who kept many hens and ducks, had never married and didn't have any family. Her one obsession in life was to help everyone else, the poor, the downtrodden, the rich. She would take her eggs to the village every day and sell them. If someone were sick she wouldna ask any money for the eggs, she would give them free. She was loved and respected in the village by everyone because they believed that henwives had supernatural powers, that, even, they could compete with the Devil!

Now the thing about the henwife was she never in her life ever went to church. And the people of the village were very upset sometimes because the old henwife had never come to church. Oh, they loved and respected her – when they were ill it wasn't the doctor they called upon. They lay in bed . . . if it was the wife, she would say, 'When the old henwife comes to the door bring her in to see me.' If it was the husband who was ill or sick, he would say to his wife, 'When the old henwife comes to the door bring her in to see me.' And you believe what I'm going to tell you, whenever the old henwife paid a visit, these people being sick or ill always recovered and felt better. Even though they paid her for their eggs or got them free.

But this old henwife who lived by the shoreside she collected driftwood that came in with the tide. Most of her time she spent carrying the wood from the beach and putting it up to dry. So this evening it was late when the henwife carried her last bundle up and placed it by the side of her little cottage. She shut up all her hens and said to herself, 'It's been a tiring day. I think I'll make myself a cup of tea.'

So the old henwife went into the little cottage, put the kettle on the fire and sat down in her chair. But then, she hadna sat for a few minutes when there came a knock to the door. She said, 'Who could this be? Probably someone in the village is ill, someone is hurt, probably someone is needing something.' She went and opened the door. There stood a tall stranger dressed in black. Now this stranger didn't have on a coat, he had a long dark cloak, a tippet, with no sleeves but holes that the arms came through. The old woman was amazed when she saw this tall dark man standing at her door.

She said, 'Sir, what's the problem, can I help you?'

'Yes,' he said, 'indeed, my dear, you can help me!'

She says, 'Won't you come in? Are you from the village?'

'No,' he said, 'not really, I'm not from the village.'

She said, 'What is wrong? Is there someone sick? Is there someone hurt? Do you need my assistance to help you?'

'No, my dear,' he said, 'I don't need your assistance. But I would like to talk to you.'

'Well,' she said, 'wouldn't it be nice if you would come in and sit down and talk by the fire?' So she brought in the stranger with his long dark tippet right to his feet. She said, 'Sit you down there by the fire.' There were only two chairs by the fireside. And he sat down by the fire. She saw he was strange, very queer, tall and dark with this flowing tippet right to the floor. She said, 'Is there something I can do to help you?'

'Yes,' he said, 'my dear, there is a lot you can do to help me. Would you let me explain myself first?'

'Well certainly,' she said, 'explain yourself, why are you here?'

'Well,' he said, 'the reason I have come to see you is, I have something to talk over with you.'

She says, 'I'm just about to make myself a cup of tea. And if you give me a few moments, the kettle's just about boiling. Would you like a cup of tea?'

'No, my dear,' he says, 'I don't want a cup of tea.'

So the old woman, her name was Jenny, she made herself a cup of tea. She took it, sat down by the fireside and put her cup on the floor beside her. 'Now,' she said, 'stranger, tell me why you're here.'

'Well,' he said, 'the reason I am here is because you are disturbing me!'

She said, 'Disturbing you?'

'Yes,' he said, 'my dear, you are disturbing and hurting me terribly.'

'Hurting you?' she said, 'I have never hurt a soul in my life.'

'Of course,' he said 'you have, maybe unknown to you, you have! Aren't you a henwife?'

'Of course,' she said, 'I have hens, ducks, geese, as you can see for yourself. But they're all shut up for the night.'

'Oh don't worry,' he said, 'I know all about that.'

'Then' she says, 'what is your problem?'

He said, 'The problem is, my dear, that you are going to the village and you are helping people.'

'But,' she said, 'it's my job to help people – that's what I do.'

He said, 'I'm talking about sick people.'

'Oh,' she said, 'are you a doctor?'

'No,' he said, 'I am not a doctor.'

She said, 'who are you?'

He said, 'I am the Devil.'

113

'The Devil?' she said, 'I don't believe you're the Devil.'

Then he pulled up the tippet and he stretched out his foot in front of her cup of tea. And there was a shiny black cloven hoof on the floor.

The old Jenny was amazed. Now she had heard wonderful stories about the Devil, but she never in her life believed there were such a thing. Now here in her very room sat the one person she never believed in. She said, 'You are the Devil, are you? And why have you come to see me?'

'The reason I have come to see you, my dear Jenny,' he said, 'is you are curing too many people. Oh, you think that by curing these people and making them healthy that you are being good. And some day you must die, and you want to go to "the other place". But do you ever give a thought – you might come to me in Hell?'

She said, 'Look, Devil, if you are the Devil as you say you are, now you've proved it to me, I've seen your hoof beside me. I am an old woman, and all my life I have set out to help people who are sick and ill. And I have worked hard, I've done everything within my power to help people. When I am old and dead and gone, I don't care if I go to heaven or go to Hell! What can you do to me if you get me to Hell?'

And the Devil smiled, 'What can I do to you, my old friend?' he said. 'The things I can do to you are unmentionable.'

'But,' she says, 'you won't be doing it to my body, will you, Devil?'

'But,' he said, 'I'll be doing it to your soul!'

'Well,' she says, 'you can have my soul.'

'But woman,' he said, 'do you understand, I am the Devil! And when you die you are going to Hell. Or maybe you think you are going to "the other place", but you see the choice is up to you. You can either go to "the other place" or you go to hell and join me!'

'Well,' she says, 'I don't care where I go to! *But my own ambition is to help all the people.*'

'Oh ho,' he said, 'I have had many people you have helped in my place, in Hell!'

'Well,' she said, 'we're not talking about the people, we're talking about you and me! What did you come here for?'

He said, 'I've come here to tell you to stop helping the people in the village, the sick ones, the poor, the elderly, the decrepit, the humble! Stop helping them, and then I will trouble you no more.'

She says, 'Devil, I'll tell you something. Listen to me. I am an old woman. I have worked all my life and I am not afraid of you. I've heard stories of the Devil, how you torment these souls in Hell. But if you ever have the pleasure of meeting me in Hell – can we sit there and talk the way we talk right now?'

'No, my friend,' he says, 'not really. When I get you in Hell, I'll torture you more than I've ever tortured a soul – because you are denying me the souls I should have!'

And she says, 'Look, I'll tell you something! I'll go on helping all the people in the village who are sick and ill. *If it prolongs their stay on earth I'll try my best – to keep them alive and as healthy as possible!* And some day when you get me in Hell you can do whatever you please with me.'

And the Devil said, 'Is that your last word?'

She said, 'That's my last word!'

The Devil stood up and he said to her, 'Well, I see. Is there no way I can convince you?'

'No way,' she said, 'Devil, you can convince me.'

He said, 'I'll tell you something, old woman, I've enjoyed being with you. And I just can't wait till I see you again! But I'll tell you – before I go – would you shake hands with me?'

And the old woman said, 'Certainly! Because I have no fear of the Devil.'

The Devil reached out and he shook hands with old Jenny the Henwife. And he said to her, 'Long may you live. Look, if you ever have the pleasure to talk to anyone about me, tell them you shook hands with the Devil!' And then he was gone.

Old Jenny lived alone in her little house by the shoreside, carried her firewood and tended to the sick for a long long time, until she died. And as the story says, I don't know if she went to Hell or went to the other place . . . but I'm sure, wherever she went she was happy.

JACK AND THE DEVIL'S PURSE

A long time ago in the West Highlands of Scotland Jack lived
with his old mother on a little croft. His father had died when
he was very young and Jack never barely remembered him.
He spent most of his time with his mother. They had a few
goats and a couple of sheep on their small croft. His mother
kept a few hens and she sold a few eggs in the village. She
took in washing and knitting and doing everything else just to
keep her and her son alive. But Jack grew up. He loved and
respected his mother. And he tried to make the croft work,
but things got very hard. The ground was too hard and stony,
little crops could he grow. He always depended on the few
shillings that his mother could bring in because he couldn't
get very much of the land. And where they stayed was about
two miles from the small village – there was a post office and a
local store and a little inn. Jack used to walk there every
week to get his mother's few groceries, or messages. And Jack
had grown up to be a young man by this time.

So one day his mother called him, 'Jack, are you busy?'

'Well no, Mother' he said, 'I'm no busy. I've cut the wee
puckle hay and I've stacked it up, it's no much.'

She said, 'Would you like to go into the village and get
something for me?'

'Of course, Mother,' he said, 'I always go, you know I
always go.'

117

So she gave him a few shillings to walk into the village. And he went into the store and bought these few groceries for his mother. He came walking across the little street, and lo and behold be was stopped by an old friend of his mother's who had never seen his mother for many years. But the friend knew him.

'Oh Jack!' he said, 'you're finally grown up to a big young handsome man.'

Jack said, 'Do I know you, sir?'

'Och laddie,' he said, 'ye ken ye know me, I'm a friend o' yer mother's.'

'Well,' Jack said, 'I've never remembered much about you.'

'Oh but your mother does! Tell her old Dugald was askin for her when ye go back!' He said, 'I was your mother's lover, you know!'

'Oh well,' Jack said, 'that's nothin to do with me.'

'Well, tell your mother I'll come out and see her first chance I get,' he said. 'I've been away travelling. But now I'm back and I'm settled here in the village, I'll prob'ly come out and see her sometime.'

'Okay,' says Jack, 'I'll have to hurry.'

'Oh no,' he said, 'laddie, ye're no goin awa like that! Come in wi me!'

Jack said, 'Where?'

He says, 'Into the inn.'

Jack says, 'The inn? Sir, I don't –'

'Dinna call me "sir"!' he said, 'call me Dugald!'

He said, 'Sir, I never was in a inn in my life.'

'Oh laddie,' he said, 'you mean to tell me you never had a drink?'

'No me, Dugald,' he said, 'I never had a drink.'

'Well,' he said, 'you're gettin one now! Come wi me.'

Into the little inn. Jack had his mother's little groceries, he placed them beside the bar.

118

'Two glasses of whisky!' Full glasses of whisky . . . 'Right,' said old Dugald, who'd had a few glasses before that, 'drink it up, laddie! It's good for ye. And I'm comin to see yer mother, mind and tell her!'

Jack drunk the glass o' whisky for the first time in his life. Oh, he choked and coughed a little bit and it felt strange to him. He had never had a drink before in his life. But after a few seconds when the warm glow began to pass across his chest and his head began to get a little dizzy, Jack felt good!

And old Duglad said, 'Did you like that?'

Jack said, 'Of course, it was good.'

'Have another one,' he said. So he filled another glass for Jack and Jack had his two full glasses of whisky for the first time in his life.

He said, 'Well now,' he was feeling a wee bit tipsy, 'I think I'd better go home wi my mother's groceries!'

'Okay laddie,' he said, 'mind my message now! Tell yer mother I'll come out to see her because she's an old girl friend o' mine!' Old Dugald was well on with drink.

Jack picked up his little bag and he walked back . . . two steps forward, three steps back. But he made his way to his mother.

When he walked in his mother was pleased to see him, she said, 'Your supper's on the table.'

'I'm no wantin any supper, Mother,' he said.

She said, 'Jack, have you been drinkin? You know, Jack, drink ruined yer father. It was drink that killed yer father.'

'Oh Mother,' he said, 'I had the best fun o' my life. In fact I met an old boy friend o' yours!'

And she touched her hair and she pulled her apron down, you know! She smoothed her apron, she said, 'What did you say, laddie?'

He said, 'Mother, I met an old boy friend o' yours!'

119

And she tidied her hair, pulled down her apron and said, 'What did you say?'

'I met an old boy friend o' yours and he's comin to see ye!'

She said, 'A, my boy friend? I have nae boy friends, laddie.'

'Ay Mother,' he said, 'you've had a boy friend – before you met my father.'

She said, 'What's his name?'

He said, 'Dugald.'

'Oh,' she said, 'young Dugald, young Dugald! God, laddie, I've never seen him for years.'

'Well Mother,' he said, 'he's comin to see you onyway.'

She was pleased about this. She'd forgot about Jack's drinking. So they sat and they talked and they discussed things. And things went on as usual. But Jack had the taste of drink.

Now every time he went to the village he would say, 'Mother, could I borrow a shilling fae ye, or two shillings or three shillings,' every time for the sake o' getting a drink. And Jack finally got hooked on drink. Till there was no money left, there was no money coming into the croft by his work or his mother had nothing to spare. She gave him what she could afford to buy the messages and that was all.

'Mother,' he said, 'gie us a shilling, or something!'

'No son,' she says, 'I havena got it.'

'Anyway,' he says, 'I'll walk to the village.'

So on the road to the village there was a crossroads, one road went to the left, one road went to the right. Jack was coming walking down, he said, 'God upon my soul, bless my body in Hell, and Devil . . .' he's cursing to himself. He said, 'What would I give for a shilling! My mother has nae money, she gien me everything she had. God, I could do with a drink! I could do, I could walk in an buy mysel a glass o' whisky and really enjoy it. *God Almighty, what's wrong with me?*'

No answer.

He said, 'The Devil o' Hell – will ye listen to me? *I'd give my soul tonight to the Devil o' Hell if he would only give me a shilling for a drink!*'

But lo and behold Jack walked on and there at the crossroads stood a tall dark man. Jack was about to pass him by when, 'Aye, Jack,' he said, 'you're makin your way to the village.'

Jack looked up, he said, 'Sir, do you know me?'

'Ah, Jack, I ken you all right, you and your mother are up in that croft there.'

But Jack said, 'I've never met you, sir.'

'No, Jack,' said the man, 'you've never met me. But I heard you muttering to yourself as you were comin down the road. And the things you were sayin I was interested in.'

Jack said, 'What do you think I was sayin?'

'Oh,' he said, 'ye talked about your God . . . and you mentioned my name.'

'Your name?' says Jack.

'Of course,' he said, 'you mentioned my name, Jack. I'm the Devil.'

'You're the Devil?' says Jack.

'I am the Devil, Jack' he said, 'And you said you would gie me your soul for a shilling for a drink.'

Jack said, 'Look, let you be the Devil of Hell or the devil of nowhere, I would give my soul to the Devil, the *real Devil* tonight!'

He says, 'Jack, I am the real Devil!'

'Ah,' Jack says, 'I dinna believe ye.'

'Well,' he said, 'can you try me?'

Jack said, 'What do I try ye for? What hae ye got to gie me? Hae you got a shilling for me?'

The Devil says, 'I'll go one better.' Puts his hand under his cloak and he brings out a small leather purse. He says, 'Jack, look, you said you would sell your soul to the Devil for a shilling for a drink.'

Jack says, 'Gladly I would.'

'Well,' he says, 'look . . . I've got a purse here and in that purse is a shilling. But I'll go one better – every time you take a shilling out another one'll take its place – and you can drink to your heart's content. You'll never need to worry again. But on one condition.'

'And what's your condition?' says Jack.

He said, 'You said you would give me your soul!'

Jack said, 'If you're the Devil you can have my soul – it's no good to me – a drink I need!'

'Take my purse,' said the Devil, 'and spend to your heart's content, and I'll come for you in a year and a day.'

'Done,' says Jack, 'show me your purse!'

The Devil gave Jack a little purse, and he opened it up. A silver shilling in the purse.

'Right,' says Jack, 'it's a deal.'

The Devil was gone, he vanished.

Jack walked to the village, spent his mother's two-three shillings to buy the things his mother needed, and he said, 'I've got a shilling in my purse.' And he walked across to the local inn. Took the shilling out, put it on the bar and called for a glass of whisky. Got his glass of whisky, drunk it up. Called for another one and drunk it up. 'Now,' he said, 'Devil, if you're telling the truth . . .' And he opened the purse, lo and behold there was another one! He spent another one, and another one took its place. And Jack got really drunk. He walked home to his mother, purse in his hip pocket. 'Now at last,' he said, 'I can drink to my heart's content.' He gave his mother her messages.

'Where did you get the money to drink, Jack?' she says. 'You've been drinkin.'

'Och,' he says, 'I met a couple o' friends, Mother.' He never told her. But anyhow, Jack made every excuse he could get to go to the village. And every time he went he got drunk as usual. Day out and day in. Oh, he bought things for his mother forbyes.

But one night after three months had passed she said, 'Jack, you've been drinkin a terrible lot. Where are you gettin all this money?'

'Ach Mother,' he said, 'it's only friends I meet.' But she was pleased with that.

But after six months, after Jack had been drinking for another three months she said, 'Jack, look, you'll have to tell me the truth. Where is this money coming from? You've been drunk now for weeks on end. Not that I'm complainin . . . drink killed your father, it'll prob'ly kill you too. You're a young man and it's none o' my business.'

'Ach Mother,' he said, 'it's only money I've been gettin from my friends, they owed it to me.'

Another three months passed, and nine months had passed. Jack was still drinking to his heart's content. One night he came home very drunk.

She says, 'Jack, do you know what you're doin? That's nine month you've been drinkin every week. Laddie, ye ken you're workin with the Devil!'

He says, 'What, Mother?'

She says, 'Laddie, you're workin with the Devil, drink is Devil's work! It killed yer father and it'll kill you.'

'But Mother, what do you mean?'

'Well,' she says, 'I'm tellin you, laddie, *it's Devil's work*. Laddie, where are ye gettin the money?'

'Well,' he says, 'Mother, to tell ye the truth, I really met the Devil.'

'Ye met the Devil?' says his mother.

'Aye, Mother,' he said, 'I met the Devil. And he's comin for me in a year's time.'

'But,' she said, 'what do ye mean?'

'Well,' he said, 'to tell you the truth, I coaxed you for a shilling and I begged you for money. I was cursin and swearin at the crossroads and there I met a man. And he gave me a purse wi a shilling in it. And I sold my soul to him. And he tellt me he's comin for me in a year and a day.'

She said, 'Laddie, where is the purse?'

Jack took the purse from his pocket and the old woman looked. It was a queer looking purse, she had never saw nothing like this before. He said, 'Look in it, Mother, see what's in it.'

And the mother looked in, there was a single shilling in it, silver shilling.

He said, 'Mother, tak it out.'

And the old mother took it out. She held it in her hand.

'Now,' he said, 'look in there, Mother!'

And she looked again, there was another one. She took another, and another one took its place. Oh, she catcht it and she clashed it to the floor. She says, 'Laddie, that's *the Devil's purse* you've got!'

'But,' he says, 'Mother, what can I do with it?'

She says, 'Laddie, get rid of it. Ye ken the Devil's got ye!'

'But,' he says, 'Mother, I've tried. I'm beginnin to understand now that your words are true. I threw it in the fire when you werena lookin, but it jumped back out again. I throw it away, it comes back in my pocket again. Mother, what am I goin to do? I dinna want to go wi the Devil.'

Now Jack began to get to his senses, he stopped drinking for a week, never had a drink. One shilling lay in the purse. He said, 'Mother, what can I do? He's comin for me!'

'Oh I ken, laddie, he's comin for ye! We ken that. You shouldna hae took it from him in the first place.'

JACK AND THE DEVIL'S PURSE

'Mother,' he says, 'help me, please! I dinna want to go wi the Devil!'

'Well,' she says, 'look Jack, there's only one thing I can tell ye. I have an old sister you've never met, your auntie and she lives a long way from here, Jack. And I was always askin ye to go and see her for a visit. She's an old henwife and people thinks that she's a bit of a witch, and if onybody can help you, she's the only one that can. Would you tak my word, Jack, forget about the purse! Tak it wi ye, show it to her and explain yer case to her.'

'But where does she bide, Mother,' he said. 'Ye never tellt me this afore.'

'Oh laddie,' she said, 'it's a long way fae here.'

'Well,' he said, 'Mother, if she can help me I'm goin to see her.'

So the old woman told Jack where her old sister stayed, and the next morning Jack went on his way to find his old auntie. And he travelled on for days and days and he finally came to his old auntie's little cottage. She had a cottage on the beach by the shoreside and she kept hens and ducks. He walked up and knocked at the door.

And a very old bended woman came out and said, 'Hello, young man! What do you want here?'

He said, 'Auntie, do ye no ken who I am?'

She says, 'What do ye mean, I'm no auntie of yours!'

He says, 'I'm Jack, I'm your sister's son.'

'Oh,' she said, 'my sister's son from the farthest point of Ireland!* I never never thought you would ever come and see me. Come in, laddie, come in! I'm pleased to see ye. And how's my old sister?'

'Yer old sister's fine,' he said, 'but it's me I'm worried about.'

* farthest point of Ireland – end of the land

'And what's wrong wi you, laddie?' she said, after he'd had a wee bite to eat.

'Well look, auntie, to tell ye the God's truth, I'm tooken over wi the Devil.'

'Oh dear me, laddie,' she says, 'sit down and tell me about it.'

So Jack told her the story I'm tellin you.

She says, 'Laddie, show me the purse!'

And she took the purse, she opened it. There was one single shilling in it. She took the shilling out and she looked again – another one took its place. She took the shilling, she put it back in, and the other one vanished. She said, 'Laddie, you're really tooken over wi the Devil, that's the God's truth!' So she took the purse and she put it on the little table. She said, 'Jack, there's only one thing ye can do. But wait a minute . . . ye can stay here the night with me. But tomorrow morning you want to go up to the village and see the local blacksmith. Tell him to put the purse on the anvil in the smiddie and to heat a horseshoe in the fire, and *beat that purse* like he's never beat anything before in his life! But I have a wee present for ye and I'll gie it to you in the mornin.'

So Jack spent a restless night with his old auntie. But next morning after breakfast she came out. She had a wee small Bible that you could barely see, the smallest Bible you could ever see! She said, 'Jack, put *that* in your pocket and don't part wi it for nobody under the sun!'

So Jack took the wee Bible and he put it in his pocket. He thanked his old auntie very much and told her he would go to the blacksmith and see him.

'Tell him I sent ye! Tell him old Isa sent ye up!'

So Jack bade 'farewell' to his auntie, walked up to the little village and came to the blacksmith's shop. The old blacksmith was busy over the fire with a bit leather apron round his waist. There weren't a horse in the smiddie or nothing. And Jack walked in, the old blacksmith was blowin up the fire.

He turned round, said, 'Hello, young man! What can I do for ye, ye got a horse with ye?'

'No,' Jack said, 'I've no horse, sir, I've no horse. I was down talkin to my auntie, old Isa.'

'Oh, old Isa!' said the blacksmith, 'oh, the old friend o' mine. Aye, what can I do for ye?'

'Well,' he says, 'I'm her nephew. And I want you to help me.'

'Oh,' he says, 'any friend of old Isa's is a friend o' mine. What can I do for ye?'

'Well,' he says, 'sir, look, it's this purse. It belongs to the Devil!'

'Oh, belongs to the Devil,' said the blacksmith, 'I see. And what am I supposed to do with it? Throw it in the fire?'

'Oh no,' Jack said, 'you'll no throw it in the fire. I want ye to put it on the anvil and beat it, my auntie says to beat it with a horseshoe.'

'Well,' he said, 'your auntie cured me many times when I was sick. And what *she* says 's bound to be true.'

So the old blacksmith took the purse and he put it on the anvil. And he went in and got a big horseshoe, he put it on a pair o' clippers and held it in the fire. And he held it till the shoe was red hot. He took and he beat the purse. And every time he beat the purse a little imp jumped out! It stood on the floor, ugly little creature with its long nails and ugly-looking face. And the blacksmith beat the purse . . . another one and another one and another one came out. Till there were about fifteen or sixteen imps – all standing there looking up with their curled nails and their ugly little faces, eyes upside down and ears twisted – they were the most ugliest looking things you ever saw! The blacksmith and Jack paid no attention to them. And then the last beat – out jumped Himself, the Devil! And within minutes he was tall and dark.

He turns round to the blacksmith and to Jack, 'Aye Jack,' he says, 'heh-h, laddie, ye thought you could beat me didn't ye? You thought you could beat me by beatin this purse! But laddie, that maks nae difference, you only beat the imps out and they're mine. And *you're* still belongin to me!'

The old blacksmith stood in a shake, he was terrified. He said, 'I-I had nothing to do with it.'

Devil said, 'Look, nothing to do with you, old man, nothing to do with you. Tend to your fire. This young man is my problem.' He said, 'Jack, you thought you could beat me, didn't ye? I've come for you, Jack, you've got to come wi me!' And all the little imps is gathered round in a knot together and they are standing there, they're watching and they're hanging on to the Devil's legs. He says, 'Jack, you've got to come with me!'

But Jack says, 'I'm no dead yet.'

He says, 'That was no bargain – I never mentioned you being dead. You told me you'd sell me your soul, so you must come with me!'

'Well,' Jack says, 'if that's it, that's it!'

So the Devil walked out from the blacksmith's shop with the imps all behind him, and Jack and he went on his way. They travelled for days and weeks through thorns and brambles and forests and places, caverns and valleys till at last they came into Hell. And there in Hell was a great cavern with a great roaring fire, and all these little cages full of imps. The Devil opened an empty one and he put all the little ones in, hushed them in and he closed the door. They stood with their nails against the cages, their ugly faces – some with faces of old women, faces of old men, ears upside down – the most ugly looking creatures you ever saw in your lifetime.

'Now,' says the Devil, 'I've got you!'

'Well,' Jack says, 'what are you goin to do with me?'

'Well, Jack,' he said, 'to tell ye the truth I don't know what I'm goin to do with you. You spent my money, ye know, and you enjoyed yourself.'

'That's true,' said Jack, 'I enjoyed myself.'

'And you tried to deceive me.'

'That's right,' said Jack, 'I did try.'

'But,' he says, 'I finally got ye. But I'll be lenient with you, Jack, if you'll do something for me!'

Jack said, 'Well?'

He said, 'I'm goin away for a long time, Jack. I must go on a journey, I have some people to see in a faraway country who are due a visit from me the Devil! And all I want you to do is to sit here by the fire and take care of the imps while I'm gone.'

'Oh,' Jack said, 'that's no problem, no problem atall.'

So then there was a flash of light and the Devil was gone. Jack was left all alone in Hell. Cages and cages all around him, a burning fire . . . all by himself.

So he sat for many hours wearied and wondering, how in the world was he going to get away back from Hell? Thinking about himself, thinking about everything else and then lo and behold, he put his hand in his pocket and he felt the little Bible that his auntie had given him. And he brought it forward. He looked at it and he opened the first page. And because he had nobody to talk to and the light was so bright by the fireside, and he was wearied, he thought to himself he would read – though he'd never read the Bible before in his life. He turned the pages and he got kind of interested. And he sat there reading and reading and reading . . . Quiet and still it was in Hell. He looked all around. All the little imps were up with their nails against the cages, and they were peaceful and quiet. They were not doing anything. Jack was reading away to himself. And then he said to them, 'Would ye like a story?'

They did not say a word.

So Jack started and he read aloud from the Bible. And all the imps gathered round their cages with their hands round the steel bars, and they were sitting listening so intent. Jack read page after page from the Bible and they were so interested. Then Jack stopped.

And the moment he stopped they started the wildest carry-on, they were screaming, they were fighting and arguing with each other and biting each other, 'Aargh!'

Jack opened the Bible again and then the screaming stopped. 'Aha,' said Jack, 'it's stories ye like isn't it?' He went round every cage in Hell and opened them all. He let them all out. And they gathered round him by the fireside. They sat on his legs, they climbed on his knees, they keeked into his ears, they sat on his head, they pulled on his ears and pulled his hair. And then Jack started reading aloud from the Bible. They sat quietly listening. And he read the Bible through and through and through for many many times. He must have read the Bible through a dozen times, and they enjoyed it. But the moment he stopped, they started arguing again and fighting! So to keep them quiet Jack kept reading the Bible. And the more he read the quieter they were. So Jack said, 'The only way that I'm going to get peace is to read the Bible to you!' So he read the Bible through a hundred times.

And then there was a flash of light! There stood the Devil with an old man on his back. And he came up and threw the old man in the fire. 'Right, imps,' he said, 'come on and get your spears, get this old man tortured!'

But they all ran behind Jack, they curled behind his legs, they climbed behind his back. And they wouldn't look at the Devil.

'Come on, imps,' said the Devil, 'the're work to be done!'

But the imps wouldn't look at the Devil in any way. Paid him no attention.

The Devil said, 'Jack, what have you done to my imps?'

Jack said, 'I've done nothing to them, I read them a story.'

'A story!' says the Devil. 'Where did you read them a story?'

'From the Bible.'

'Take *that* from me,' said the Devil, 'take that from me, put that away from me!' He says, 'Jack, you're no good to me. No good to me, I'm sorry I ever even thought about you in the first place. Jack, you're too bad for heaven and you're too good for Hell. Look, I'm goin to give you a chance. You take all these imps and go and start a place for yourself! I'll set you free. Now be on your way! And *that's* the road to take,' there was a space o' light. And Jack walked on.

'Good-bye, Devil,' he said, and he walked on through the space o' light and travelled on. Lo and behold all the little imps, one after each other followed him in a single file till he disappeared from the cavern o' Hell! When the beautiful sun was shining he landed in a beautiful forest. And he sat down there, he wondered, 'Am I really free from Hell?' he said. 'Will the Devil ever bother me anymore?' And all the little imps gathered round him. They sat on his knees, they sat beside him. And Jack said, 'Well, little fellas, we have a problem. You know I've led you from Hell. Now I canna take you back to my mother in any way. But look, this is a nice place for you to live. Go out in the forest and be good and kind and create in your own likeness, and enjoy yourselves. Make a home for yourselves here, you'll never need to go back to Hell again!'

And then the little fellas vanished in the forest.

Jack walked on to his mother's. And his mother was pleased to see him.

'Did ye do what I told you, Jack?' she said.

'Aye, Mother, I did what you tellt me, and have I got a story to tell you!'

So the little imps lived in the forest and they spread out and they created in their likeness. And therefore began the legend of all the goblins and elves and gnomes in the land. And Jack lived happy with his mother. But he never took another drink, and that is the end of my story!